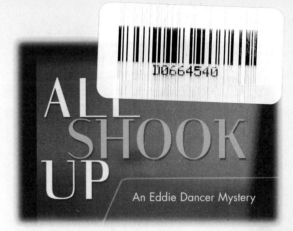

ALL
SHOOK
UP

An Eddie Dancer Mystery

ALL SHOOK UP

An Eddie Dancer Mystery

Mike Harrison

ECW Press

Published by ECW PRESS
2120 Queen Street East, Suite 200, Toronto, Ontario, Canada M4E 1E2

NATIONAL LIBRARY OF CANADA CATALOGUING IN PUBLICATION DATA

Harrison, Mike (Mike S.), 1945-
All shook up / Mike Harrison.

(An Eddie Dancer mystery)
ISBN 1-55022-688-6

I. Title. II. Series: Harrison, Mike (Mike S.), 1945– .
Eddie Dancer Mystery.

PS8615.A773A64 2005   C813'.6   C2004-907047-9

Cover and Text Design: Tania Craan
Production and Typesetting: Mary Bowness
Printing: agmv

This book is set in Minion and One Ioda

The publication of *All Shook Up* has been generously supported by the Canada Council,
the Ontario Arts Council, and the Government of Canada through the
Book Publishing Industry Development Program. Canadä

DISTRIBUTION
CANADA: Jaguar Book Group, 100 Armstrong Avenue, Georgetown, ON L7G 5S4

UNITED STATES: Independent Publishers Group, 814 North Franklin Street,
Chicago, Illinois 60610

PRINTED AND BOUND IN CANADA

ECW PRESS
ecwpress.com

Dedication

This book is for my beautiful wife Janet, and for Alec and Annalisa, Gavin and Shauna, and, of course, my Mum, my brother Martin and his family, and my sister, Norma, and all of her family

And for my Dad who's always looking over my shoulder.

Thank you all for believing.

Special thanks to Kelly McLachlan and Andrea Piper, my lovely lady readers. Thanks also to absolutely everyone at ECW Press.

A nod and a wink to Detective Greg James, who will understand when he reads the book.

And last but not least, thanks to the gifted Sarah Carson. The mistakes that remain are all mine, not hers.

Chapter One

I TACKLE THE *Calgary Herald* crossword in my office every day. I call it my office, though others have called it considerably less. It's an upstairs single room in a two-storey brick building that offers spectacular views of the parking lot out back. And a shared bathroom. The rent's not cheap but looking down on all that high-end Japanese plastic comes at a price. I was working on today's crossword puzzle. In pen because I live on the edge. I'd just inked forty-three across, CHARISMA, when someone swung open the office door without knocking.

He was somewhere in his forties, a tall, hard-built man in very tight black pants and a tight black leather vest with nothing under it. Silver chains hung from his belt and disappeared into various pockets. Several heavy rings decked his fingers but there was no wedding ring. Who'd have him? Jet-black hair swept back with a walnut-whip twirl at the front. The sideburns were long and cut on the angle. He looked like an Elvis impersonator on a coffee break. On his well-defined left bicep was an ornate tattoo. A long dagger with a wavy blade that disappeared down the throat of a snake. It looked crisp and fairly new. He glanced at me sitting behind the desk, pulled the door open again and read my name embossed on the glass.

"That you?" He pointed to my name.

"That be me. Who be you?"

"What?"

"I'm Eddie Dancer." I stood up. "I didn't catch your name."

"Joe Baker."

"Take a seat, Joe Baker."

I was being cruel. I wanted to see if he could sit in the skin-tight pants, from the cut of which I surmised he probably wasn't Jewish. He remained standing.

"You the private-eye guy?"

"That be me."

"Right." Only he said "Roit." He shuffled his feet, unsure what to say next.

"You need a private investigator, Joe?"

"Yeah."

"Okay."

"So how's this work?"

"Well." I took pity on him. I stood up, came around the desk, hitched myself to the corner. "Have a seat." I nodded to the opposite end.

He lowered himself onto the far corner and crossed an ankle over his knee. He wore black, Cuban-heeled boots that were in fashion around the time of the Cuban missile crisis. And he rode a motorcycle. I know that because I'm a detective. It says so on my office door. Also, the top of his left boot was badly scuffed but the right boot was unmarked. Motorcyclists change gear with their left foot. One down, five up. The gear changer messes with the leather. Mine sure does.

"So," he began. "I need you to find someone. His name's Richard Wyman. We did a bank together. He took off with my share of the money."

"By doing a bank together, you mean what, you renovated it?"

He raised an eyebrow.

"What d'you think I mean?"

Score one for Joe Baker.

"When?"

"Soon as you can."

"No." I shook my head. The spoken word wasn't Joe's strong point. He needed visual aids. "When did you do the bank, Joe?" I figured he was the one who had done the time and was hoping Richard Wyman hadn't spent his share of the money.

Fat chance.

"Last Friday."

I stood up.

"Whoa." I held my hands out front like I was warding off a mad dog. "That's really more than I wanted to know. You can't tell me you just robbed a bank."

"Why not? You're a private eye. I tell you stuff it's like privileged information, right?"

"Wrong." But quaint. "That's between you and your lawyer. And maybe your priest but definitely not your private eye guy."

"Ah, shit."

"Shit indeed."

"So what happens now?"

"Nothing."

"I just told you I robbed a bank."

"I once stole candy from a grocery store. Now we're even."

"Huh?"

"Joe. You tell me you committed a crime, I'm supposed to report it."

"You gonna turn me in?"

He looked belligerent and when his bicep twitched, the snake seemed to swallow more of the knife blade.

"No, Joe. I'm saying, if I know a crime's been committed, I'm supposed to report it. I'm not saying I'm going to report it. Just don't go giving me any details, okay?"

"Well." He looked uncertain. "How you gonna find the guy I'm looking for if I don't give you details?"

I didn't have the heart to tell him I wasn't going to help find his missing partner-in-crime. I was stalling for time.

"Hypothetically," I said.

He rolled his eyes. "Hypothetically, we knocked over the Bank of Canada last Friday. I got the shaft. Richard Wyman disappeared with all my money."

"What happened to honour among thieves, Joe?"

"I've asked myself that a thousand times," he said and I believe he had. "So. What's it gonna cost for you to find him?"

I saw my way out without risking my licence, being locked up or having Joe Baker flex his biceps in my direction again.

"Two thousand a day plus expenses," I said with a straight face.

We can all dream.

He looked at me for a long moment. "If I had that kinda fuckin' money, I wouldn't need you, would I?"

"First five days up front," I added, in case he wavered. "In cash."

"Yeah?" He straightened up so fast, his chains rattled. "Well screw you, Mister Fuckin' Money Bags!" He strode towards the door, unable to resist a final zinger over his shoulder. "If I had your fuckin' money, I'd burn mine!"

Phew!

His Cuban heels clicked smartly across the floor, out the door, along the hall, down the stairs to the sidewalk and out of my life forever.

I wish.

Chapter Two

TWO DAYS LATER, things began to get a little weird around the office. A painting crew arrived that morning, and set up ladders and paint trays in the hallway before disappearing for the traditional three-hour painters' lunch break. At noon, I slipped across to The Sub Palace for a foot-long and a Coke. I was eager to get back out of the heat. It was pushing thirty-two degrees. That's about ninety degrees in the real world. Not that my office has air conditioning but at least my office had a fan.

I went back up the stairs and down the short hall. My building is a hundred years old, a Heritage site. It's in Victoria Park, just north of the world-famous Stampede grounds. Which probably explains the rent. The company that owns the building was smart enough to leave the exterior walls of brick, giving the place a very funky look. I'm next door to a music composer we call The Kid and across the hall from a graphic design studio that does creative work and printing for most of the bars and nightclubs in the city. Frequently, late at night, one of the bars sends over a "thank-you" case of cold beer for a job well done and, if they aren't there, it's left with me for safekeeping. I'm not sure the studio is aware of this arrangement but The Kid and I sometimes crack a cold one.

The hallway was empty but the door to my office was ajar. Not that I'd bothered to lock it, but as a precaution, I transferred the Coke to the same hand that held the foot-long to give myself a free hand. In the ten years I've been a private eye, I've come across a few people who didn't like me. Go figure. I stepped quietly into my office. A large man was sitting in the client chair, his head down, long arms dangling between his thighs. At the risk of sounding sexist, he looked pussy-whipped. The whippee stood next to him, her arms folded beneath her breasts, her face set in concrete, the mouth a thin, bloodless line that looked liked it had been drawn in charcoal. She wore a short-sleeved, faded yellow blouse over a shapeless brown skirt.

I walked behind my desk and set down my lunch.

"You're here to see?"

"The detective," she said without warmth.

I smiled at her.

"You have an appointment?"

That flustered her.

"No." She stepped forward, then stepped back again. She played with a tiny crucifix on a chain around her throat. "Do we need one?"

I made a big show of checking my watch, like it mattered.

"I guess I can spare you a few minutes."

"You're . . ." She glanced back at my door. "The detective?"

"Yes." I didn't stand up. "And you are?"

"I'm Sue-Ann Wyman. This is my husband, Dick."

I looked at Dick. "Dick." He looked up. "That would be short for Richard?"

"Yeah."

Richard Wyman.

"I'm Eddie Dancer." I stood up and extended my hand. He stood up, came over. Six four, six five, about two hundred and forty pounds with a handshake like a pit bull. He wore blue jeans and a blue denim work shirt. His arms were long and thick, like an ape's. His head was completely devoid of hair. He wasn't just bald but hairless. A hairless ape. His eyebrows, the few hairs he did have, were pale blond and almost invisible. His eyes were sharp blue. He travelled in a toxic cloud of after-shave; the sort men buy for three bucks a bottle, thinking women enjoy not being able to breathe. After the handshake, he sat down again. His wife didn't move.

"How can I help you, Mr. Wyman?"

"Dick."

"Dick."

"We need you to find someone," Sue-Ann said.

"Okay."

"Don't you want to take notes?"

I tapped the side of my head.

"Like a steel trap."

"Well." She looked at her husband, unsure how to proceed.

"He or she? This person you want me to find?"

"He," she said.

"Does he have a name?"

She looked down at her husband. Clearly, he had no wish to be part of this.

"His name is Joe Baker," she said.

It figured. I stopped her right there.

"Mrs. Wyman. I don't think I'm going to be able to help you."

She blinked, a startled look.

"You can't?" she said. "Why not?"

She pronounced her *w*s with an eff up front, so she actually said "Fwhy?"

"Conflict of interest," I said.

"What do you mean?"

"My interests are being conflicted. Specifically my interest in staying out of jail."

She stiffened.

"Who's going to jail?"

"Not me." I turned to Dick. "Are you the same Richard Wyman that robbed the Bank of Canada with Joe Baker last Friday?"

Richard Wyman came out the chair way too fast for a guy his size. He didn't bother going around the desk, just came over the top looking to strangle me. I stood up fast and moved sideways. I clamped my hand over the back of his neck and shoved his head down hard onto the desktop. I picked up a long, thin letter opener and stuck the sharp end in his ear.

"Christ! That hurts!"

"It's meant to," I said, reasonably. "Behave yourself."

I looked at his wife. She hadn't moved but she looked very angry.

"Dick!"

The sound of his name ricocheted around the room like an angry bullet. He stopped thrashing and I relaxed my hand on the back of his head but left the letter opener where it was.

"All right ! Get that thing outta my ear!"

I obliged but kept hold of it in case I needed to open the mail. Or slit his throat. He slid off the desktop and massaged his ear with his pinkie.

"I take it that was a yes," I asked him.

"What was?" He was belligerent.

"Yes, you robbed the Bank of Canada last Friday," I prompted.

He looked at his wife, sheepishly.

"How'd you know?" he said.

"I'm a detective. It says so on my door. You're looking for Joe Baker because?"

"He took off with my share of the money."

"There's no honour among thieves anymore, Dick."

"You can say that again."

"Dick." I spread my hands. "I can't help you."

He looked at me with raw suspicion.

"How'd you know about the bank?"

"Joe Baker told me."

The look on his face was worth it.

"You know Joe Baker?"

"I know Joe Baker."

"And he told you about the bank job?"

"Yes. A slightly different version to yours."

"Yeah?"

"In his version, you're the one who ripped him off."

"He's a lying bastard!"

He was on his feet again. I waggled the letter opener and he sat back down but it was the look from his wife that really withered him. He sank further down in the chair.

"What did he want?"

"He wanted me to find you."

"What the hell for?"

"I told you. He wants his money back."

"So where is he?" he demanded.

"No idea." I shrugged. "He didn't like my fee. He stormed out. No forwarding address."

Dick's face went dark and I was afraid he might burst a blood vessel. Sue-Ann took charge before he boiled over.

"Mr. Dancer." She laid a hand on Dick's shoulder like a restraining order. "I, we, want you to find Mr. Baker in order to recover the money stolen from the bank. Not, as you might expect, to recover my husband's share of the proceeds for ourselves, but to return the money to the bank." She paused. "Are you married, Mr. Dancer?"

Married? I wasn't even dating but I saw no need to explain that. "No." I shook my head. Sadly, because that's what she seemed to expect.

"Well, sometimes spouses do very foolish things, Mr. Dancer. My husband did a very foolish thing. He is a good man but he can be easily led. Joe Baker took advantage of my husband's good nature."

"Your husband may still have to face the authorities," I told her.

"If it's at all possible to keep his name out of it, Mr.

Dancer, it would be very much appreciated. We have three young children and it would make life very difficult if their father was sent to jail." She glanced over at him. "Again."

"I understand," I said.

"We will pay your usual fee. Plus, if you recover the money, I'm sure the bank would see fit to pay you a reward."

"How much are we talking here, Dick?"

For a brief moment, his face flushed the colour of absolute inner pride.

"Two hundred and fifty thousand dollars."

Phew.

"I, we, are very anxious to put this behind us, Mr. Dancer."

I leaned forward, my elbows on the desk, chin on my fists. It was only the fact that they planned to return the money that made me decide to to help them. "Let's do this," I said. "Everything you tell me is in the strictest confidence. Whether I decide to take the job or not, it goes with me to the grave. Word of honour." I made the sign of the cross. It seemed like the Christian thing to do.

They exchanged a look and Sue-Ann, her lips compressed tighter than lockjaw, gave a single nod. Richard Wyman sat forward, his long, hairless arms dangling between his legs, and he proceeded to tell me more than I ever wanted to know.

Chapter Three

IT ALL BEGAN FOUR WEEKS earlier when Dick Wyman received a phone call from Joe Baker, a man he'd never met. To gain Dick's confidence, Joe dropped the names of various people with whom Dick had spent quality time in the slammer.

"Which prison?" I asked him.

"The Barbary," he said and I nodded. The Barbary is a hard-time federal prison about an hour's drive northwest of the city.

"For what?"

"Same thing. I robbed a bank," he said.

I nodded and let him continue.

Joe Baker told Dick he was looking for a partner to pull off a bank job. A foolproof bank job. Dick was reluctant but Joe convinced him to meet and he outlined the plan. It was, as Joe had claimed, damn near foolproof.

Joe Baker would phone the bank manager of the Calgary branch of the Bank of Canada, claiming to be an investment broker affiliated with the Bank of Canada in Toronto. He would purport to represent a man named George Duncan.

"George was an actual lottery winner," Dick explained. "We got his name out of the paper. Five million bucks. He took off for the Bahamas the same day he picked up his winnings."

According to the way Joe would tell it, George was moving, not to the Bahamas, but back to Calgary, his hometown, to deposit his winning cheque with the Calgary branch of the bank. Since George was interested in investing in the Alberta economy, the manager of the Calgary branch would be in a better position to assist George than an investment broker in Toronto.

Joe and the bank manager would firm up the day and time for George to meet. Since George was a vintage car buff, he would be adding to his collection right away and would require a couple of hundred thousand, say a quarter of a million, from his winnings, in cash, to pursue his hobby.

"My job was to keep the bank manager's wife company," Dick said. "She was expecting someone to tune her piano. She had one of them big ones, a grand, you know?"

Clearly, Joe Baker had done his homework.

Once in the bank manager's office, Joe "George Duncan" Baker would reveal that there was no winning lottery cheque and the bank manager would be told to make like E.T. and phone home. Dick would answer. His message to the bank manager would be simple. Unless he gave George Duncan the quarter million in cash, Dick would chop the bank manager's wife into five million pieces.

And that's how it went down.

"Fifteen minutes after the manager phoned home, Joe

Baker phoned me. He had the money. We were to meet at Westbrook Mall. I waited five hours. He never showed."

Oddly, the robbery never made the news. Fearing copycat crimes, no doubt, the media had been kept in the dark. I looked over at the pair of them. Sue-Ann remained standing during the entire story, playing with her crucifix the whole time.

"Okay," I said at last. "Here's what I'll do. I'll find Joe Baker for you. I'll ask him to meet with you. If he's got the money and if he agrees to hand over your share, I'll return it to the bank, no questions asked. The bank won't pay a reward unless I also hand over Dick. That won't happen. You'll cover my professional fee and any reasonable expenses incurred. Is that acceptable?"

"How much is your fee?" she asked.

"A flat fee of a thousand dollars," I said. "That will buy you one week."

She squinted, adding and subtracting in her head. "If it takes longer?"

"It won't."

"But if it does?"

"It's on the house."

"And less?"

"A flat fee's a flat fee."

"I just need to understand," she said, sniffing. "Money's tight."

They murmured between themselves a while, then she wrote me a cheque in her tiny handwriting.

"Is it all right if I postdate it a few days? I need to pull some money together."

"That'll be fine."

She balanced the account, and then pushed the cheque across the desk towards me.

"You can reach us at the phone number on the cheque."

I nodded and put the cheque away in my drawer without looking at it. I thought it was the classy thing to do. We all stood. An awkward moment passed as they tried to decide whether to shake hands with me. Finally, Sue-Ann stepped forward and extended a crisp, dry hand into mine. I closed my hand around hers and it lay like a tiny dead sparrow in my palm.

"Thank you," she said.

She took her hand back and gave Dick a "follow-me" with her chin. He loped out of my office behind her like an overgrown, disjointed puppy.

I tried not to jump in the air and click my heels. I was employed again.

Chapter Four

I BEGAN IN EARNEST the following morning. Joe Baker wasn't in the Calgary phone book. There was a Jeremy Baker and a John Baker, but no Joe Baker to be found. And I thought there'd be what, thirteen? He could be shacked up, of course, and the phone could be in someone else's name. On a yellow legal pad, I wrote down what I knew of Joe Baker. That took care of the first thirty seconds.

I could go to the cops, call in a few favours, have them pull Joe Baker's driving licence but the risk was too high. Suppose they were looking at Joe Baker for the bank robbery? They'd sweat me until I bled over that one. I knew he rode a motorcycle but that really didn't help much.

There was one other way I might track him down.

The tattoo on his bicep.

The knife and the snake were unique enough that I might be able to find him through the tattooist who inked it for him. If he'd had it done locally, that is. Tattooists are a strange breed. Many have their own designs that others won't copy. There were twelve tattoo parlours listed in the yellow pages. I jotted down the addresses. They were scattered to all four corners of the city. Calgary's one of the easier cities in the world to get around. There are four quadrants that include the city centre. The centre's laid out in a grid formation, a big oblong. If the city is a lollipop, the stick up the middle is McLeod Trail, a six-lane highway of car dealers, motels, massage parlours, furniture discounts stores, muffin huts and gas bars. It's busy twenty-four seven. Calgary went from Cow Town to an international centre that never sleeps, right after the '88 winter Olympics.

I folded the list of addresses into my pocket and looked out the back window of my office. My bronze Chevy Blazer stood baking in the hot sun. When I moved into the building two years ago, I was a month behind the hookers who'd taken over the street out front. At first, they left me pretty much alone. I politely refused their offers of a good time and went about my business. Their pimp, a mean little scrawny guy they call Hot Wheels, drives a black Cadillac convertible with white upholstery. He has oversize chrome wheels with hubcaps that keep spinning after the car has stopped. Blue sex-lights under the chassis and a ridiculously loud stereo. One day, he got it in his head that I was an undercover cop. He hates cops almost as much as they hate him and he began to harass me. For the most part, I ignored him but he had this one real mean little habit that I found hard to ignore. Every few weeks, he'd wheel that damn great Caddy into the parking lot and park right behind my Blazer. He'd leave it there for hours. I couldn't drive forward because there was a row of concrete blocks that were too close to the fence line. There wasn't enough room between the blocks and the fence to drive out. The parking authority wouldn't tow him because he was on private property. I didn't own the building so I couldn't get a private tow truck to haul his ass out of there either.

One day, I decided enough was enough. I got to the office around five in the morning and spent the next two hours moving the entire row of concrete blocks ten feet back from the fence. I used a crowbar and brute strength and worked up a fine sweat but I got the job done. The parking lot was plenty big enough to accommodate the change and I parked the Blazer in my usual spot. Later that same day, Hot Wheels rolled into the parking lot, stereo blasting. He pulled up so close, our bumpers touched. He turned off the ignition, powered up the top, locked the car and left.

I gave him five minutes, then locked the office and went out back to the parking lot. I put the Blazer in four-wheel drive and drove up and over the concrete block. There was just enough room to turn the Blazer in the newly created space between the concrete blocks and the fence. I parked up, leaving the Caddy sitting in the middle of the lot. Then I took the crowbar out of my trunk and levered the heavy concrete blocks over to his car. It took me the better part of an hour, but by the time I'd finished I had moved eight parking blocks, one each front and back of all four wheels. If he tried to drive away in either direction, he'd high centre his Caddy on the concrete. As I worked, I was aware I was being watched. A Hot Wheels' hooker, a very young girl in a tiny white miniskirt and red tube top, watched me from beyond the fence. When I finished, I dropped the crowbar in my trunk and climbed behind the wheel. She approached the driver's side window.

"He'll know it was you," she said.

"You think?"

"Yeah." She nodded seriously. "But not from me," she said.

She looked me in the eye. She was achingly young and stunningly beautiful.

"Thanks," I said.

She stuck her hand through the open window.

"I'm Angie," she said and her small, white teeth looked almost too perfect. Like baby teeth.

We shook hands. It felt strange. I've never shaken hands with a hooker before.

"Eddie Dancer," I replied.

"I know who you are."

I found out later her street name was Crayola. I figure she must have had a lock on all the pedophiles. During winter, she would sometimes stop by the office if I was working late. She'd warm up but never stay for more than ten or fifteen minutes. She'd just sit quietly until the shivers ran out. I looked out for her the best I could, brought her hot chocolate in the cold, iced cappuccinos in the heat. We never talked much. I pretty much guessed her story anyway. Rotten home life, abusive parents, never going back. To her credit, I never saw her doing drugs, never saw her drunk or stoned, though how she could do what she did without mind-altering chemicals in her veins, I'll never know.

And in all that time, she never propositioned me.

Not once.

Dammit.

I just might be losing my touch.

Hot Wheels got the message, though. After that, he parked somewhere else and we settled into an uneasy truce.

Staring down at the parking lot, I knew it was just too damned hot to take the Blazer. I keep my motorcycle in the lockup at the end of the building. A silver-grey Honda sport bike. Honda named it the Blackbird. It can hit sixty miles an hour from a standing start in three seconds on dry pavement. It'll hit one hundred miles an hour in six seconds. Tweaked for top end, it can hit two hundred miles an hour on the dyno. The personalized licence plate reads "ZEN." Some people just don't get it. Dan Walsh, the world's greatest bike journalist, once said that owning a motorbike is like owning a Beretta, half a million in cash, and a forged passport hidden under the floorboards. It's a great escape route.

My escape route took me north, across the wide Bow River, enjoying the rush of wind across my face. I wore jeans, a white T-shirt and a pair of Alpinestars racing boots. If I fell off, at least my ankles would still look pretty. I hit the first parlour a few minutes after ten that morning. It was a dingy place in a basement off Edmonton Trail. A brass bell jangled as I pushed my way into the parlour. A very large and heavily tattooed woman with green eye shadow and pink spiked hair was reading her horoscope. The place smelled of disinfectant.

"You'll have to wait. I'm sterilizing the stuff."

"No rush. I'm looking for someone can do a real nice job for me."

"Sure," she said, without looking up.

"I'm thinking a curly dagger going down the throat of a snake."

She paused a moment, glancing up at me. I thought I saw something move behind her eyes but couldn't be sure.

"Sounds complicated."

"Yeah?"

"Have a look through the book, see something you like in there, maybe I can do that instead."

The book was six inches thick. It would take me an hour.

"I seen it before on a guy. Wondered if maybe there'd be someone who specializes in that design, you know?"

"Yeah. Maybe. Dunno. You wanna look or not?"

"You haven't done anything like that yourself? On the bicep?"

"No."

"You'd remember though?"

"Yeah."

"Okay. Have a nice day now."

She watched me leave without a word. I emerged in sunlight wondering why anyone in their right mind would allow someone with spiky pink hair to ink them for life.

The rest of the morning went by with about the same lack of success. I did learn a couple of tattooist jokes I'd never heard before though. "Eagle? I thought you said beagle," was funny but my favourite was, "Two Os in Bob, right?"

Around two o'clock, I'd crossed off nine of the twelve. The tenth was in a run-down section just six blocks from my office and one street south of the bus barns. Old, clapboard houses crowded each other down both sides of the street.

Almost no front yards. Most of the parked cars looked terminal. I could see the top of the bus garage from the street.

A pair of Harleys was parked out front, leaking oil as Harleys do. I parked next to them and hung my helmet from the right foot peg. A huge, mean-looking dog lay under the stoop, tied to the corner post. If it weren't so damned hot, he'd have come out from under and stood his ground. As it was, he growled but didn't move.

My boots clunked on the aging wood as I went up onto the stoop. The front door was open so I pushed aside a purple curtain and stepped into a small front room littered with mismatched furniture and a threadbare carpet. The place stank of stale cigarettes and body odour.

"Hello?"

Nobody answered. I ducked behind another curtain, this one brown with grease. I was standing in a darkened room. A big chair was bolted to the floor, the sort you'd find in a dentist's office back in the sixties. An overturned footstool lay beside it. A long counter stood against the far wall with an array of bottled inks and a sink with a leaky faucet. Cables hung from the ceiling, supporting the tattooists' motor-driven needle. I looked away. I couldn't stand needles. On the far end of the counter lay several design books, greasy photos of the artist's work, held together with Scotch tape.

"Anyone here?"

He came through a door in the back wall. Skinny as a jackal and twice as mean. I'd guess he was about fifty but it was hard to say. He hadn't shaved in a week and his long grey hair was tied back beneath a black do-rag. Even in this heat, he wore a denim jacket with the sleeves cut off and there was a buck's worth of grease beneath his fingernails. His upper arms were well defined, skinny but hard-cut with long, ropey muscles. A cigarette dangled from the corner of his mouth, the smoke squinting his left eye. He had a permanent, self-contained air of menace about him.

"You the artist?"

He turned around, arms spread as if to say, "You see anybody else here?" The world needs more comedians. Except this guy wasn't funny. A biker club patch had been ripped from the back of his jacket. How much of a badass do you need to be to get kicked out of a badass motorcycle club?

"I'm looking for something special," I said.

"Appointment only."

"Sure. When's a good time?"

"Phone first."

"Got a card?"

He considered me, then pulled a ratty-looking wallet from his jeans and thumbed a card from inside. It just said LEN with his phone number scratched out and a new one written in pencil. In case he needed to change it again.

"Can I see your work?"

"What for?"

"Like I said, I'm looking for something special. Want to know if you can do it."

"I can do it."

"You don't know what I'm looking for."

"Don't matter."

"It's a dagger going down the throat of a snake. Dagger's got a wavy blade."

He took the cigarette from his mouth and stared at me, a hard, cold stare that would have unsettled me, had I been the unsettling sort. He looked back at the door he'd just come through.

"Yo, Doug!"

A moment later, Yo Doug shuffled in. He was wider than the door and came in sideways, wiping greasy hands on a rag that he tucked in his jeans. Grease smeared his broad forehead and sweat stuck the Harley T-shirt to his massive frame. A shock of dirty blonde hair escaped his do-rag. He was maybe twenty years younger than Len and two hundred pounds heavier, most of it fat but not all of it. But it wasn't his size that caught my eye. It was the tattoo on his bicep. A dagger with a wavy blade going down the snake's throat.

"There you go," I said. "I want one just like that."

"You being funny?" Len curled his lip.

"*Moi?*"

"You soft fuck, you ain't done time." Len's voice had dropped an octave.

I turned to Doug.

"So it's like an old boys' club, is it? Spend time in prison in Bum-Fuck, Alberta and Lennie here gives you the snake tattoo?"

"Who the fuck're you?" Doug had a voice like a gravel truck.

Len moved around the chair towards me. Doug didn't need to be told twice. He came around the other side.

"I'm a private investigator. A gumshoe. A private dick."

"Yeah?" Len wasn't impressed. He grabbed his crotch. "Dick this, motherfucker."

Doug reached me first. At six feet nothing and one eighty soaking wet, I'm not likely to scare anyone but the elderly and infirm. But I do have fast reaction times. Very fast. And I do know a lot of dirty tricks and that creates oodles of self-confidence. If you're going to take on someone with oodles of confidence, you're going to think twice before mixing it up. Unless, of course, there's two of you and neither of you gives a crap about oodles or the psychology of confidence.

Then it could mean real trouble.

Doug telegraphed an overhead right hook to my jaw and I stepped under it, reaching behind his rib cage. I grabbed as much of the skin and fat that hung around his kidneys as I could. I dug my fingers in deep and tried very hard to tear the flesh from his bones. He screamed very loudly but I was expecting that because I'm told it's excruciatingly painful. He went up on his toe points like a ballerina and I twisted the skin counter clockwise. His legs buckled and he crumpled backwards to the floor. Len had to move around him to reach me and Len was more than a little pissed.

He reached for me, going for the throat. I let him come in close then finger-poked him in the eye. It hurts like a son of a bitch. It's called the Rinky-Dinky-Little-Finger-Poke but it's only funny if you're the one doing the Rinky-Dinking. Len swore viciously and came back at me. He was a tough son of a bitch. I snapped a finger into his other eye and he staggered back, floundering before tripping over the upturned footstool.

While Len and I were dancing, Doug had clawed his way back to his feet and he came at me, head down for a cannonball run. I moved back and grabbed the big chair that was on a floor-mounted swivel. I swung it towards him as hard as I could and the metal edge smacked across his shins. He went down in a heap. I put my foot on the chair and swung it hard in the opposite direction, catching Len a good one to the head.

"I've changed my mind about the tattoo," I told them. "The customer service here really sucks."

I ducked around the greasy curtain, stepped outside and jumped down from the porch, stopping just long enough to rip the spark-plug leads from both Harleys. The dog was all for ripping out my throat but the restraining rope held him back.

It was his lucky day.

I fired up the Honda, stuffed my head inside the helmet and rode away, wondering if maybe people were right when they said I could sometimes be a royal pain in the ass.

Chapter Five

CLEARLY, LEONARD AND DOUGLAS, the biker-wannabes, would find me. Like an idiot, I'd told them I was a private detective so it wouldn't take those two dimwits more than a few days to track me down. I parked the Honda in the lock-up before heading back up to my office. I locked everything that needed locking, left my office phone call-forwarded to my cell phone, double-locked the office door and headed round back to the Blazer.

I needed a safe house to crash for a while. Who you gonna call? Nosher and Splosher. They were brothers. Identical twins. They owned an old farmhouse on ten acres of treed and rolling countryside about twenty minutes southwest of the city. They bought the place from a couple of retired teachers. It came with a small guest cabin they call the Poetry Shed. The husband had entertained young men there. He'd told his wife they were poetry students. When she found out it wasn't just poetry that was getting lyrically waxed, she took him to the cleaners. I'd gone to ground there once or twice before, and Nosher and Splosher were always very accommodating.

Their real names are Brian and Ryan Newfield but don't ask me who is who. They were born in London, within the sound of Bow bells, making them true Cockneys. They came to Canada in the late seventies when things in England got a little too hot for them. They'd made a very nice living noshing and sploshing old MG TC sports cars, those little two-seaters, usually red, with raised fenders and a spoke wheel attached to the trunk lid. From the mid-sixties until they left England ten years later, they bought up every MG TC they could lay their hands on and if it wasn't for sale, so much the better. They kept the ones they paid for at their lockup in London's East End. Those they hadn't paid for were kept in a secret lockup a few miles away.

England's weather played havoc with the bodywork of the little sports cars and it was Nosher who refined the art of sculpting body filler, or "noshing," to cover the ravages of rust. Smart buyers came with magnets and attached them to the bodywork. If the magnets fell off, they knew the cars had been noshed and weren't interested. Nosher got around that by mixing iron filings with the bonding agent.

"Sploshing" was the art of slapping a fast coat of shiny new paint on the car and there was nobody better with a spray gun than Splosher. They boasted about a further refinement that involved something called Bri-Nylon, a synthetic material used to make, among other things, men's shirts. One Bri-Nylon shirt, buttons removed and stuffed into the gearbox of the little sports car, did wonders to quiet a noisy gearbox. The heat from the engine melted the Bri-Nylon, coating the gears in sticky goo.

"Good for five hundred miles," Splosher boasted.

It was the next five hundred you had to watch out for.

The bruvvers always had their eye on the main chance, which happened to arrive when a visiting American fell in love with the little red MGs and bought three, offering them a premium if they would arrange to have them shipped, by sea, to New York. "We Yanks just love 'em!" he'd said. The light bulb went on. Within a month, they accompanied their first shipment of twelve MG TCs across the Atlantic aboard a creaky cargo ship. They had placed an ad in the *New York Times* and sold all twelve right off the dock, cash on the barrelhead, their return on investment a whopping eight hundred percent.

They stayed in New York for a week buying used Firebirds and Camaros and shipped them back to the British Isles to be sold to Americans serving on American Air Force bases in the UK.

It was an incredibly profitable business. All cash, nothing to declare and between them, during a ten-year period, they shifted over five hundred MG TCs to the United States. They finally fled to Canada when the police discovered their cache of unpaid-for vehicles in the secret East End lockup.

They bought the acreage within a year and began a car repair and tow truck business. It was fairly legit though they had been known to tow a car, remove its engine, replacing it with a faulty one and tow it back from whence it came, all before the sun came up. It was all a game to Nosh and Splosh. Nefarious they might be, but when the chips were down, there are few people I'd trust more than those two. I trusted them with my Blazer last year. They removed the six-cylinder motor and shoehorned in a V-8, adding spacers to push the wheel out and give me more stability at high speed. They added headers and a dual exhaust, re-curved the distributor and replaced the clutch springs with ones that kick me in the kidneys when I tread on the gas to kick it down a gear. They rewired the light switches so I could follow someone at night without them realizing. The headlights and spotlights went on or off independently so I could mix and match a variety of patterns.

I called them on my cell to make sure the shed was available.

"Anytime, mate," Nosher said.

Or maybe it was Splosher.

I swung by my townhouse in fashionable Marda Loop — for I am nothing if not trendy — and quickly packed a sport bag with everything I might need for a stakeout and a week on the run. My first port of call was to be the rooftop of the bus barn. If I could see the roof of the garage from Len and Doug's place, I'd be able to see their place from the roof of the garage. My plan was to watch and wait, which wasn't much of a plan. But it included a little B and E, for excitement, since I needed to get into their house again without them being there. I grabbed a camping chair from the back deck and emptied my fridge. From the cupboard above the fridge, I took an unopened bottle of Ballantines in case the weather turned cool. Or in case it stayed hot.

It was still hot when I drove the Blazer back downtown to the barns and parked in the visitors' parking lot. I took a clipboard with me and walked around making notes. If anyone asked, I planned to say I was working up a quote to paint the place, but nobody asked. I moved around unchallenged and found what I was looking for on the far side of the building. A safety ladder that led to the roof.

I grabbed it in both hands and shook it. It was solid. I went up hand over hand as quickly as I could. It was a flat roof with a two-foot wall around the edge. I hurried to the south side and peeked over.

There was only a partial view of Len and Doug's place on the next street. When I moved to the left about thirty yards, I was directly opposite their house and I could see the front door clearly. Only one of the two Harleys was parked outside. I moved back to the ladder, checked that no one was looking and climbed back down. The sport bag and the camping chair lay across the back seat and I carried them to the base of the ladder. It was around seven-thirty in the evening by then and I was getting a little hungry. I threw the sport bag over my shoulder and quickly climbed back up the ladder, dropped the bag over the parapet and clambered back down for the chair.

By the time I reached my spot on the far side, I was sweating in the heat. I opened a bottle of water that had been in my fridge and took a long, cold drink. I'd made myself a sandwich for supper and I chewed through a beef and cheese on brown with Dijon mustard. From my perch, thirty feet up, I could even see the roof of my office building in the distance. I positioned the chair close to the wall and hunched down so I could see Len's front stoop without needing the binoculars. I saw something move past the front window a few times, a shadow, nothing more. Nobody came out front, nobody stopped by to visit.

By ten that night the light was beginning to fade. I needed to take a leak and I was considering my options when I heard a sound.

Leather on metal and the jangle of keys.

I glanced over at the ladder that protruded three feet above the sidewall. It was vibrating. I watched the top of the ladder. About ten seconds later, a man's head appeared above the roofline. He was wearing a flat peaked hat, the sort that security guards wear. I sketched him a wave.

He didn't wave back.

I thought it more prudent to meet him halfway, out of sight of Len's place. I moved unhurriedly across the hot, flat roof. He cleared the top rung, straightened his uniform and strode over to meet me. He was in his mid-fifties and surprisingly fit to make that climb without being winded. He wore a thick moustache that completely covered his upper lip. I wondered how his wife felt about that.

"Hi," I greeted him.

"What are you doing?" Official brusque with a touch of curt.

"Surveillance," I answered.

"For whom?"

"The Stampede Board."

"But why up here? This is Transit property."

"We're trying to catch a firebug."

"Nobody told me about it."

"I would hope not. It's supposed to be very hush-hush. Not even the media know." I'd had plenty of time on the roof to improvise. "Someone threatened to burn down a bunch of houses earmarked for the Stampede expansion. Guess someone doesn't like being evicted."

"You're on your own?"

"Up here I am but there's half a dozen of us out there." I waved vaguely over the rooftops.

"You have some ID?"

I pulled out my wallet, flipped open my ID. He took it, read every word.

"You're a private detective?"

"Yep."

"Working for the Stampede Board?"

"Yep. I guess you could phone them. Talk to Sully. I'll probably lose my job though. It's supposed to be confidential. How'd you find me?"

He looked surprised, a touch flattered.

"I didn't find you," he admitted. "I check this roof most nights. The two goons working this shift are scared of heights and never come up here. You surprised the hell out of me to be honest."

"Well, you do good work," I said.

"You're sleeping up here?"

"I'm not paid to sleep."

He considered that.

"Anything we can do to help?"

"We?"

"Well, me. I guess if it's secret, I'd better keep this to myself."

I breathed a sigh of relief.

"That's appreciated," I said.

"Gary Marshall." We shook hands, an odd ritual for two guys on a rooftop. "How long are you planning on staying up here?"

"'Till we catch him."

"That could take a while."

"I'm used to it. Got food and drink for a few days. Lots of caffeine."

He rubbed his heavy moustache with a finger, then dug around in his pocket and pulled out something on a long, thin chain.

"You'll be needing this, then."

"What is it?"

He grinned.

"The key to the executive washroom."

Chapter Six

IT WAS PAST MIDNIGHT when things began stirring at Len's place. They received a visitor. A black Caddy with the top down, the white upholstery almost luminous in the moonlight. Someone sat in the passenger seat. A girl. She stayed in the car while Hot Wheels went inside. I sat forward in the chair. It creaked loud enough to wake the dead but no one could hear above the din of the Caddy's stereo.

Hot Wheels came out, turned off the motor and pulled the girl out onto the sidewalk. I scoped her with the binoculars. It was Angie. Crayola. Hot Wheels dragged her inside the house. Clearly, she did not want to go. I waited. They didn't stay long, less than five minutes. When the door opened, Hot Wheels looked out, checking the street both ways. Then he reached behind him and dragged Angie out. An entirely different Angie. This one stumbled, falling against him. He pushed her away and I saw her reeling, totally unsteady on her feet. Something was very wrong. Her face looked slack, her jaw hung open and her head rolled from side to side as though her neck were made of rubber. Blood trickled from her nose. Her limbs seemed disconnected. She looked burned out, drugged beyond belief. Hot Wheels guided her roughly towards the Caddy, opened the passenger door and pushed her roughly inside. Len and Doug came out behind him. He high-fived them both and said something. They laughed, an evil sound that carried on the still night air. He moved around to the driver's side, climbed in. Brake lights flared red. He blew the horn and gunned the Caddy down the narrow street. Len and Doug watched him leave before they went back inside.

What the hell was that all about? I wondered what kind of drug was powerful enough to render Angie almost comatose in such a short space of time.

Around one-thirty, a light went on in the house two doors to the right. It was a bedroom light, overlooking the street. The drapes were open. A very stout woman walked past, followed by a man without his shirt. The woman turned. She was naked from the waist up. Her long, pendulous breasts hung down as she bent forward and removed a pair of industrial-strength panties. Her huge stomach hung over her thick, gray thighs.

Mercifully, the man turned off the light before I threw myself off the roof.

I sat up the whole night. Around four, I dozed off but the camping chair dug into the back of my legs and I woke half an hour later, stiff and sore all over. I stretched, my joints popping like firecrackers, and then I continued watching the house.

Nothing moved.

Around six-thirty, the sound and smell of a dozen

different breakfasts wafted my way. Bacon sizzled somewhere across the street. Toast burned as toasters popped
and eggs were boiled, fried and scrambled, along with my
stomach. Calgary is an early rising city. Already, oil company executives were at their desks and secretaries were
powdering their noses and powering up their computers for
another day in the trenches.

My stomach rumbled. If things don't improve soon, I
might have to give all this up and go find a real job.

Chapter Seven

MY CELL PHONE VIBRATED at nine-fifteen that morning. I glanced at the number displayed on the backlit screen.

Bingo!

It was Len's number. The one written in pencil on his business card.

"Hello . . ."

"You motherfucker, I know who you are."

". . . and thank you for calling the Eddie Dancer Detective Agency. Your call is important to me. If you'll leave me your name and number after the beep, I'll call you back."

"Fuck!"

The phone went dead before I gave him my impression of a beep. I gathered my belongings and hurried back to the ladder. I went over, the camping chair in my teeth, the sport bag over my shoulder. With luck, I wouldn't be back. As I turned to go, I took the unopened bottle of Ballantines from the sport bag and stood it on the roof beside the ladder. I put the key to the executive washroom beside it. It was the least I could do. I really hate lying to honest folk.

I stowed everything in the Blazer, then ran back up the ladder and dropped down behind the wall. A quick peek confirmed the Harley was still there.

I hit the redial button.

It rang four times before Len answered.

"Yeah?"

"Good morning, sir," I said, polite as ever. "This is Eddie Dancer. Sorry I missed your call. I was picking up the mail. I'm back in the office now, how may I help you?"

The line went dead. I peeked over the rooftop and watched as Len and Doug came running out of the house less than a minute later. Doug cranked the lone Harley upright and put everything he had into the kick-start. It fired first time and Len climbed on the back. I was already down the ladder as the Harley roared along the narrow street. I jumped the guardrail around the parking lot and sprinted across the road, flattening out against the far wall as the Harley turned onto my street and picked up speed. They roared past me, heading over to my office. I ran hard across an empty lot that spat me out three doors down from their house, then ran across the street, past the mad rat dog tied beneath the stoop. I avoided the front door, not wanting to start the damn dog barking any worse than he already was. I ran down the side of the house, hoping to go in through the back door but there was no back door. They had built a garage right off the back of the house. At the end of the garage, there was an up-and-over door, but it was locked. On the far side I found a filthy window hung with a thick, heavy blanket. The garage was close to the fence and it was a tight squeeze, the ground littered with bald tires and cans overflowing with rancid oil.

The window was locked.

I popped the latch with my knife, making no more noise than a freight train hitting a cement truck. I struggled to open it, then hauled ass over the sill. I left the window open and dropped the blanket back in place.

I was in the lion's den. In broad daylight. And in virtual darkness. The damned curtain cut off the only available light.

I held my arms in front of my head, hoping not to walk into anything sharp. It wasn't my head I should have worried about. I smacked my shin on something solid, bolted to the floor. Cursing, I hobbled towards the far wall, found a light switch and flicked it on. A forty-watt bulb threw a mean light over the garage. Len's Harley sat near the overhead door, a mess of wiring still hanging from the distributor. From the reinforced rafters hung a greasy block and tackle on a heavy chain. It was the sort of equipment you'd need to remove an engine from a motorcycle. In the corner I saw six or seven such engines. Stacked against the wall away from the window were the bike frames. Harley frames. The thing on the floor that had smacked me in the shin was a paint stirrer, beside it an airless spray gun and a small compressor. On the workbench lay a hand-held grinding wheel, perfect for grinding off vehicle identification numbers or VIN tags. Close by was an old tobacco tin almost full of VIN tags from dead motorcycles. I was in a chop shop. On impulse, more out of curiosity than anything else, I grabbed a bunch of the metal tags and stuffed them in my pocket.

I stepped through the door into the back room and found the light switch. The dentist's chair sat in the middle of the room. The tattoo book was still on the shelf in the far corner. I flicked quickly through the pages, aware that Len and Doug could return at any moment. Some of the photos were so old, I could hardly see the image. I stopped, took a deep breath, visualized the tattoo on Joe Baker's bicep. I remembered it looked fairly clean, fairly new. I flipped to the front of the book and worked my way towards the back.

I was barely a quarter of the way through when I heard the unmistakable sound of a Harley. I froze, ears super tuned to the sound that split the air like a jackhammer. It rose, then slowly fell, moving away from me.

I doubled my efforts to locate a picture of Joe Baker. About halfway, I found what I was looking for. Two photos. One of the tattoo, the other of Joe Baker flexing his bicep, showing it off. I peeled the photos away from the page. On the back of both someone had written Joe B.

That was it. No phone number. No address. Just Joe B.

Not Joe Baker. Just Joe B. Like they knew Joe Baker well enough not to need to write his last name. I replaced the photos and dropped the book back where I found it. I hunted around for something like a Rolodex. Time was rushing past me and they must know I wasn't at the office by now. I heard another noise.

Another Harley.

The Rolodex wasn't anywhere to be found. I was getting desperate. I figured it would be near the phone but I couldn't find that, either. Then I had a bright idea. I took out my cell phone and hit redial. It took a few seconds, then somewhere, a phone began to ring. I was in the wrong room. I ducked through the greasy brown curtain into the front room. The phone was on the floor. Next to it, down beside the sofa, was a black address book, the cover thick with grime. I grabbed it, flicked it open to the *B*s. Nothing. The sound of the bike was louder now. It was coming my way. Loud pipes save lives. I was really hoping that was true.

Under the *J*s I found Joe B with a phone number. After his name, there was another letter *B*. I studied the phone number carefully, committing it to memory before snapping off the light. The front window rattled as the Harley pulled into its parking spot outside the house.

I ducked under the brown curtain, hit the light switch, ran to the garage, memorized my route to safety and snapped off the forty watt light as the front door opened. I heard voices twenty feet behind me.

In darkness, I groped for the blanket over the window. The voices were louder now. They were in the next room. I found the blanket, flicked it aside and swung my legs over the sill, ducked my head and dropped to the ground, hoping like hell not to land on anything sharp. I pushed the blanket back down as the light came on behind me.

The hell with the window. I left it open and scurried away like one of Ali Baba's forty thieves.

Chapter Eight

I PICKED UP THE BLAZER from the parking lot where I'd left it and risked a drive-by of my office. Everything looked normal. I pulled a U-turn and drove slowly back down the block, parking a few doors down from the entrance, leaving the doors unlocked in case I needed to leave in a hurry. It was already hot outside and the weather forecast predicted another scorcher. The street door to my office building was propped open. The guys in the studio looking for some airflow. I took the stairs carefully, scanning the corridor, ears pinned like a Doberman's.

Nobody. Not even the painters.

I stepped around a tall stepladder and reached my office door, tried the handle. The door was locked. I debated going in when a movement at the end of the hallway caught my eye. I turned quickly. Two people came out of the washroom.

Maybe Len and Dougie had called for backup.

I moved toward them, the element of surprise on my side for a few seconds longer. Then I stopped. They were just girls. Skinny girls and one was having problems staying upright.

"Angie?"

She was propped against the wall. Dried blood crusted beneath her nose. Her head flopped over on her shoulder. Her eyes were open but they kept rolling back in her skull. She looked awful. The other girl was a hooker I'd seen around from time to time but I didn't know her name.

"She's real sick," the girl said. "She needs a doctor."

I moved closer. Drool ran like a string of pearls from the corner of her mouth.

"What's wrong with her?" I asked.

The other girl shrugged.

"Dunno. She's been like this all night."

"Are you working?"

"I'm always working."

"Do you have time to come with me to the hospital?"

She shook her head quickly.

"He'll kill me."

Her eyes looked huge.

"No, he won't. Come on, take her left side."

We managed to walk her to the front of the hall. I had to move the ladder, cursing the painters. Her feet wouldn't work properly so I carried her down the stairs.

"My Blazer's right out front," I told the girl. "Go open the door for me."

The girl looked even more scared. She looked up and down the street several times, then darted over to the Blazer and pulled open the rear door. I hurried behind her, laid Angie across the back seat and ran around to the driver's side. I climbed in, motioning the girl to do the same. After a moment, she clambered in next to me. I fired the engine and pulled away from the curb.

"I'm taking her to the Rockyview Hospital. I'll need you to stay with her."

"I am so dead."

"Then don't come back."

"I have to."

"If he is going to hurt you, why go back to him? Stay with Angie. She needs you."

"He'll find us."

"No he won't. I know a place you can stay. It's out in the country."

"I'll help you get her to hospital but then I gotta get back."

I drove fast through the downtown traffic, cutting back between lanes and ignoring anything but red lights. She was silent beside me.

"I'm Eddie," I said when we cleared the downtown.

"I know."

"What's your name?"

"Velvet."

"Your real name."

"Velvet."

I let it go at that. I checked on Angie every few minutes. She wasn't doing well. Her breathing was ragged, her movements jerky and spastic.

I spun the back wheels as we took the corner up to the Rockyview. The emergency parking lot was almost full but I managed to find a vacant stall. I left Velvet with Angie while I ran for a wheelchair. I wrestled her in it, fighting to keep her upright. She looked completely out of it. I pushed her through the sliding doors, jumping the queue at the admitting desk, catching a head-to-toe look of disapproval from the triage duty nurse.

I don't like hospitals. They smell awful and they are full of nasty things. Like needles. And sick people. I parked the wheelchair alongside the triage desk, ignoring the muttered complaints from the walking wounded behind me.

"She needs help."

"Name?"

"Angie."

"Last name?"

"Don't know."

"Address?"

"Don't know that either."

"Social insurance number?"

"All I know is her name."

She gave me a look. Nurse Ratched. But much cuter.

"What's the problem?"

I looked down at Angie. She looked like she was in a coma.

"I don't know. I think somebody drugged her."

Nurse Ratched looked over at Angie, then back at me. "Right." She came around the desk and checked Angie's vitals.

"She's a hooker," I said, like that was a surprise. "She works the street outside my office. I found her like this in the hallway this morning. I think she's been like this since last night."

"Go wait in the waiting room."

"For how long?"

She shrugged. "A while."

Mike Harrison

47

"You're going to have to do better than that."

She made eye contact. Her eyes were green with flecks of amber that glowed like burnished gold. Her blonde hair was cut short, almost spiky, like a pixie. She looked tired.

"We see girls like this all the time. They mix their drugs until they get a brain freeze. Sometimes, they forget to breathe. No oxygen for three or four minutes. They suffer irreparable brain damage. There's nothing much we can do for them."

"I don't think she takes drugs."

"And I'm Michael Jackson's mother. Take a seat."

I wheeled Angie over to a row of seats while Nurse Ratched scribbled on a pad. Velvet was getting restless.

"Listen, Velvet. Can you stay with her for little while longer? I have something I have to take care of."

"He'll kill me. I'm dead already."

"Then stay. I'll be back soon and I'll take you somewhere safe. Both of you."

I thought she was going to cry but she bit her lip and moved her head in what might have been a nod. I doubted she had the resolve to stay long.

"Here." I scribbled down my cell number then, as an afterthought, I added Nosher and Splosher's phone number. If you can't reach me, these are friends of mine. Mention my name. They're good people."

I gave her the note and left quickly, before she changed her mind.

Chapter Nine

I COULDN'T USE MY CELL phone in the hospital. I walked around back, away from the traffic, and sat on one of the benches alongside the footpath. The view was breathtaking. The back of the hospital faced west, overlooking the Glenmore Reservoir. A patchwork of rolling foothills and the vast expanse of the Rocky Mountains formed a glorious backdrop. Nobody could stay sick very long with a view like that.

The phone glowed iridescent blue as I powered it back up. I tapped in the number I'd memorized for Joe Baker and pressed SEND. Some days are diamonds, some days are stones. It was answered on the third ring.

"Yeah?"

"Joe?"

"Who's this?"

"Eddie."

"Eddie who?"

"Eddie the detective Dancer."

"Oh, Eddie the fuckin' millionaire fuckin' detective Dancer. How'd you get this fuckin' number?"

"I found Dick Wyman."

"The fuck you did."

"Joe, I'm not kidding. I found him. He's agreed to meet you."

"What's this shit? You're setting me up. You're fingering me for the fuckin' job."

"I'm not setting you up, Joe. If I was, why didn't I just give the cops your cell phone number? They could run you down in three minutes flat and have a SWAT team on your ass three minutes after that."

"Yeah?"

"It's your call. You pick the time and place, I'll be there. If you're okay with that, then I'll take you to meet Dick Wyman."

He thought about that for a while.

"You talk with him about the money?"

"Yes."

"What's he say?"

"You'll have to talk with Dick. I can't speak for him."

"Why should I trust you?"

"Because I'm pure of heart. Do you have a better idea?"

He was silent on the phone.

"You came to me," I reminded him. "Now pick the place."

"Lemme think about it. Maybe I'll call you."

"You've got my number?"

But he'd already hung up.

I wondered if God would forgive the lie about me being pure of heart.

Chapter Ten

I SAT AND ENJOYED THE VIEW for a while. The wind off the mountains was warm and friendly. I wasn't born in Calgary. Like most people, I came from somewhere else. When I first saw the mountains, I thought they were twenty minutes away, driving slow. I figured I could walk to them in an hour. A few weeks later, I rented a car and drove west. I drove for two hours before I reached them. Life. It's all about perspective.

Nurse Ratched looked up from the front desk when I went back to Admitting. She nudged her head an inch to the right and I stepped aside to meet her as she came around the desk.

"We've taken blood samples. We couldn't find any needle tracks. Doesn't mean she isn't doing drugs, she could be ingesting or inhaling. She's presenting symptoms of probable brain damage. We won't know anything for a few hours. Leave me your phone number."

I looked back over my shoulder, searching for Velvet.

"She left," she said.

"Ah. A friend in need."

I gave Nurse Ratched my card. She read it.

"You can call the desk anytime," she said. "We get busy, maybe somebody forgets to call you."

"Thanks." I held her there simply by not moving away. "What are her chances?"

"Of what? Playing the violin? Lousy."

"Of recovering," I said.

"Even worse."

"You said you've seen lots of girls like this."

"One or two a month. Street kids. We do what we can but we don't know what drugs they are on. Your friend's pretty bad." She reached out and touched my arm. "She's incontinent."

"Oh."

"In case you were thinking of taking her home with you."

"No." I shook my head. "I have a place she can stay, though. She'd be safe."

"She'll need round-the-clock care."

"For how long?"

"What part of this aren't you understanding? Her condition is probably permanent."

Spoken like a death sentence.

"Oh, Christ."

"I have to go. I've been off duty for over an hour."

When she'd touched my arm, I saw she wasn't wearing a wedding ring. That's the sign of a good detective. Or of a desperately single man.

"Coffee?" I asked her.

"There's a machine down the hall."

"No. I mean, can I take you out for coffee?"

She looked at me anew, her head cocked to one side.

"You hitting on me, Eddie?"

I was pleased she remembered my name.

"Maybe."

"I'll take a rain check. I have to get home, feed the cat."

Nurse Ratched? Nurse Nightingale, more like. Her name tag said Cindy. I watched her walk away, hips incredibly slim beneath her nurse's uniform. I thought about what she'd said.

Incontinent.

Forever.

And I knew that somebody was going to pay the price.

Chapter Eleven

IT WAS TWO DAYS BEFORE Joe Baker called me back. I'd driven out to Nosher and Splosher's place, endured their warm and friendly ribaldry when I arrived, including, "Fuck me, look wot cat dragged in."

I phoned the hospital several times a day but there was no change in Angie's condition. Her brain had swollen and she was on round-the-clock medication to keep the swelling to a minimum. They were considering drilling her skull and removing part of it to relieve the internal pressure but, since there was little brain activity, they decided against it. She was a vegetable.

To keep from going stir crazy, I offered to chop wood to help the boys through the coming winter. I attacked the logs with a vengeance, splitting many of them with a single pass of the axe blade. I sweated profusely and drank endless cups of cold water drawn from the well. By the end of the first day, I was surrounded by mountains of lumber. Chopped into manageable pieces, they would fit the airtight stove. I checked my cell phone for messages. Nothing urgent. I delayed a few jobs, turned down two others. That night, I showered until the water ran cold. The Poetry Shed is a single room with a chesterfield, a small table, two chairs, a fridge, a small stove and a double bed. The bathroom was an afterthought, accessible, not through the room itself, but all the way around the rear of the building. As afterthoughts go, the bathroom ain't half bad, as the boys would say. A huge jetted tub, a two-person shower, a low flush toilet and two sinks. It's done in grey and white Italian marble. It raises the bar for gay poets.

I climbed into bed and closed my eyes. I didn't think I'd fall asleep easily and I slept fitfully. I dreamt of huge, mechanical beasts that smelled of hot oil and I shivered as the shadowy creatures sniffed my skin. Deep red eyes glowed like coal as they slithered through my darkness. I awoke three or four times until, suddenly, it was daylight. A radio played softly outside. Led Zeppelin. "Stairway to Heaven."

I hoped that wasn't an omen.

After another shower, I joined the twins for breakfast. They never asked why I was holing up or from whom. I'd helped them once, years ago, and had thus achieved the elevated status of "mate." If you're British and you're some-body's mate, you're much more than a friend, far more than a buddy, even more than a spouse. A mate is nothing less than a life-long blood brother.

That morning, breakfast was the same as it had been for the last forty years and would be for the next forty, if they lived that long. Eggs, bacon, sausages, fried tomatoes and fried bread. On Sundays, they added mushrooms and occasionally pancakes. They covered everything in ketchup or, as they called it, tomato sauce. They drank instant coffee made from milk and something called chicory. It wasn't as bad as it sounds. Okay, I'm lying, it was awful. Afterwards, they would let out an enormous belch and sit back with their hands folded over their stomachs, happy as clams, content to let the world pass by until they got back to work.

While they did what they did in their garage, I went back to chopping wood. My hands were blistered and I'd borrowed a pair of gloves to carry on splitting the atom.

At first, everything ached, especially my shoulders, but once I'd worked up a sweat and flushed the lactic acid from my system, I fell into a nice rhythm. Chop-rip-stack-bend. Around mid-afternoon, I stopped to pile the wood in the woodshed where it overflowed in all directions.

"Penance, is it?" Nosher asked as he happened by.

"What do you care?" I asked him.

"Don't give a rat's arse. They'll burn either way."

By nightfall, I was truly exhausted. I swallowed a couple of Tylenol, drank four beers with the guys and soaked my aching body in the jetted tub. Nosher gave me a box of baking soda.

"Put 'alf a box in the baff water."

After my soak in baking soda, I was surprised to find I ached far less than I had expected. Score one for baking soda. I climbed into bed early and slept like a baby until dawn. I showered, dressed and went for a long walk to clear my head. My morning call to the Rockyview confirmed Angie's condition remained unchanged. Nurse Nightingale was off that day but her colleague told me they were making arrangements to transfer Angie to a long-term care centre.

They promised to let me know when and where she would be going.

Joe Baker finally phoned me after breakfast. He wanted to meet. Under the bridge where Highway 22X crosses Highway 2. Eleven that morning. He'd be parked on the hard shoulder in a light blue Chevy truck.

"Come alone."

Click.

Not big on conversation is Joe.

Chapter Twelve

I DROVE EAST ALONG HIGHWAY 22X, since that was the quickest way into the city from the acreage. The mountains in my rearview mirror appeared smudged in the heat. I turned north onto Highway 2, pulled a fast U-turn at the first set of lights and drove south as instructed. It was ten minutes before eleven and Joe's truck was already parked beneath the bridge. I had phoned Dick Wyman and told him I was meeting Joe but I didn't say where, just told him to make himself available at short notice.

The blue Chevy was empty. The doors were locked. I peered in the windows. I looked up and down the highway but could see no sign of Joe.

"Dancer!"

I looked up. Joe Baker was standing on the bridge above me. He waved me up the steep embankment to the right of where I'd parked. I locked my doors and scrambled up the steep slope. Chopping all that wood must have been good exercise because I was only gasping, not wheezing, by the time I reach the road. I guess it was Joe Baker's way of making sure I wasn't being followed.

He walked over to a white panel van with its motor running and slid the side door open. The interior was empty except for a small pile of clothes. He tossed me a pair of jeans, a white T-shirt, some Fruit of the Loom underwear still in its packaging and a worn pair of sneakers.

"Put those on," Joe said. "Leave your own clothes on the side of the road."

"I could be arrested for this," I said but I understood his concern. He wasn't taking any chances that I had a bug on me. I did as he asked, stripping down until I was completely naked.

"You wanna search me?" I asked him.

"Get dressed, asshole."

"Getting a little homophobic, Joe?"

"Little. Yeah, that's right. Remind me never to call you a big dickhead."

The jeans were a bit loose and the runners a bit tight but overall it wasn't a bad fit. I climbed into the passenger seat and Joe pulled onto the road, heading east. I wondered what anyone would think if they came across my discarded clothes by the bridge. Would they think it was a suicide? A naked jumper? But where's the body? I bet he landed in a cattle truck. That's how urban legends get started. Someone hijacks you, makes you take off all your clothes, throws you off a bridge and presto — you're an urban legend, eaten by a pack of hungry cows.

"What's the plan, Joe?"

"The plan is, you keep your fuckin' mouth shut until I tell you to open it. I still don't trust you so we're gonna ride around awhile until I'm sure we aren't being followed."

"You're lousy company when you're pissed," I told him.

He glared at me. He was still wearing all black but with a few more chains. Joe Baker's bling-bling. I wondered if he would quiver his bicep at me again. I pushed the seat back, closed my eyes and dozed while Joe backtracked and lane-switched and ran red lights until finally, half an hour later, he was convinced we weren't being followed.

"Okay." He nudged me awake. "There's a Tony Roma rib place about a mile down the road. They've got an outdoor patio. Call Wyman. Tell him to meet us there at one o'clock. He comes alone. I spot anyone, anyone at all, game's over." He reached down beside his seat and pulled out a gun. "I ain't going back to jail."

I phoned Dick Wyman and gave him Joe's instructions. "Come alone. We'll be on the patio."

I didn't tell him Joe was armed and dangerous. No need to inflame him and have a shoot out at the O.K. Corral.

Joe wore a lightweight black cotton jacket to conceal the gun. We walked across the parking lot and took a seat on the outdoor patio. Joe sat with his back to the restaurant so he could watch the parking lot. When the waitress came, we ordered a cold beer and read the menu. She came back, flipped a pair of coasters and put the cold beer in front of us. We ordered pizza.

It was past one o'clock by the time we'd finished eating. Joe was getting fidgety, looking at his watch. By ten after, he'd had enough.

"Let's go."

He stood up. I drained the last of my beer. I stood up and

turned around and saw Dick Wyman walking towards us across the crowded patio. He was wearing a jacket.

"Who the fuck's that?" Joe demanded as Dick came closer.

"It's Dick."

Dick slowed, scowling at me. He pulled up, six feet from our table. His after-shave made my eyes water. His hand went beneath the jacket.

"Who's that?" Dick asked, pointing at Joe Baker with his free hand.

"Who the fuck are you?" Joe asked, his hand round the handle of the nine mm pistol in his waistband.

I looked from one to the other.

"Are you guys kidding me? Dick, this is Joe Baker. Joe, this is Dick Wyman."

"You call yourself a fuckin' detective?" Joe snarled. "This guy ain't Dick Wyman."

"And you ain't Joe Baker," Dick countered.

Joe looked insulted. "What you talking about? I'm Joe Baker, you asshole. Who the fuck are you?"

"I'm Dick Wyman. You might be Joe Baker but you ain't the Joe Baker I'm looking for." He turned to me. "Joe Baker's black, you asshole."

"Yeah," Joe said, sneering. "So's Dick Wyman. Black as fuckin' coal."

We stood glaring at one another for several long seconds. Joe Baker was a black man. So was Dick Wyman. I thought about that, then, in a flash, I understood what had happened.

"You've been duped," I told them.

"We've been what?" Joe still had his hand on his gun.

I tried again.

"You've been fucked. Both of you. There never was just the two of you in this thing. There was always a third guy. You just never knew it."

They stared at me, a long silence broken only by the sounds around the patio. Finally Joe turned to Dick Wyman.

"You got my money?" he asked.

"I got diddly shit," Dick said. He sat down at our table and I noticed the way the hot sun glinted off his bald head. "Sit down." He turned to me. "Get us a beer. We need to talk."

I ordered three more beers.

When I sat down, I made sure my chair was a long way from Dick Wyman's. His after-shave could do serious damage to a man's lungs.

Chapter Thirteen

IT WAS OBVIOUS, NOW, what had happened. A third party, whom Joe referred to as "that black bastard motherfucker," had contacted each of them purporting to be the other. Three men, but only two of them actually committed the robbery. The third man planned the whole thing, then stepped in and stole the money.

"How'd he do that?" Dick wanted to know.

"He lined up a car for me," Joe explained. "A black Trans Am. I left it half a block down from the bank, hood up, trunk open so I wouldn't get towed. I came out, threw the money in the trunk and took off. I was supposed to switch cars in the Bay parkade, top floor. When I got there, I couldn't open the fuckin' trunk. The key didn't work. Plus the getaway car wasn't there. I tried to jimmy the trunk but it wouldn't open."

"He switched cars on you," I said.

"Yeah. I left some gum in the car, on the passenger seat. Wasn't there when I got back in. Should have known then, I guess, but I wasn't thinking 'bout no gum."

"You should have waited with the car." Dick scowled at him.

"I did. Waited maybe an hour up on the fuckin' roof. Then the cops came. I think he tipped them off. I climbed down the outside of the fuckin' ramp. Coulda killed myself. Waited around for fuckin' hours. Went back up there again, the car was still there. I was gonna try an' jimmy the trunk again but this time I saw a fuckin' wire. Red, 'bout this long." He held his fingers an inch apart. "Figured it was a booby trap. Looked inside the car. My gum was back on the passenger seat. He'd switched cars again and he'd taken the money car."

"Son of a bitch!" Dick smacked the tabletop. A few diners glanced over then looked away quickly.

"I take it you checked out the plates?"

Joe gave me a withering look.

"When'd you last see him?" I asked him.

"Friday morning. We had breakfast, went over everything one last time. He left first, paid for breakfast. Wasn't too happy about it, either, but I didn't have my wallet. Like I carry ID when I'm on the fuckin' job."

"How'd he pay for it?"

"What?"

"The breakfast."

Joe frowned. "Credit card, I think."

"You're sure?"

"No, I'm not fuckin' sure." He scowled again. "Yeah. I remember now. The pen didn't work. He was shaking it. The cashier gave him another one."

"Where were you?"

"Ralph's Place on Seventh Avenue."

I knew the place. I'd had breakfast there myself a few times.

It was worth a shot.

Besides, it was the only lead I had left.

Chapter Fourteen

RALPH'S WAS HALF FULL when I walked in an hour later. It was all dark wood, polished brass and those hanging plants that the Beautiful People called fronds. Joe had driven me back to the bridge to retrieve my clothes. I kept my Fruit of the Looms on. Getting naked in front of Joe Baker again didn't do much for either of us. I had his cell number and told him I'd be back in touch.

I parked at a meter and walked to Ralph's Place. I waited for the hostess to spot me. Her name tag read Margo. I gave her my card and asked to see the manager.

"He's busy," she said. She never even looked at my card.

"Aren't we all?" I said, then, "Revenue Canada."

She scowled and hurried off to the back of the restaurant. I followed her, passing through a swinging door to the kitchen, then down a short hall to an office out back. I walked in behind her and heard her say "Revenue Canada" like I was contagious.

The manager saw me. He was a Pakistani gentleman with short black hair and a crisp white shirt. His name tag said Ali. He steepled his beautifully manicured fingers and looked at my card on the desk in front of him. His desktop was immaculate; the only things on it were a monitor and a mouse.

"Thank you, Margo," he said quietly.

I stepped aside as she brushed past me.

"That Margo. Such a kidder."

His face remained blank. Obviously not a Superman fan.

"How might I help you, Mr. Dancer?"

I looked around for a chair, hoping to take a moment to bond with him, but there was only one and he was in it. I sat on the edge of his desk.

"Do you have the receipts from last Friday morning by chance?"

"And why would you be asking?" he said.

"I'm working a credit-card fraud. Two men came in for breakfast last Friday. They paid with a credit card we believe to be fraudulent."

"We?"

"Visa."

"You work for Visa?"

"Visa, Master Card, American Express, Diner's Club." I shrugged, the big-time private detective.

"What is it you want, Mr. Dancer?"

"I need you to find that receipt."

"And what is it that you wish me to do with it, assuming I can find it?"

"I'll buy it from you. Face value."

He shook his head. "I cannot do that."

"Why not?"

"Last Friday's revenue has already been entered in the books, Mr. Dancer. It would take a considerable amount of work for me to change such an entry. It is the computer, you see."

"It might save you a court appearance when we catch him. And an audit."

He paused.

"I would very much like to help Visa, Mr. Dancer, but what you ask is time-consuming."

"But not impossible?"

"Very few things are impossible, Mr. Dancer. Just expensive."

Aha.

We agreed on a hundred bucks. While he pulled down a filing box and rifled through it, I told him what Joe Baker and the man claiming to be Dick Wyman had had to eat. He calculated the amount in his head, then pulled a copy of a credit-card receipt and smoothed it out on the desktop.

"The man you're after is not only a crook, Mr. Dancer. He is also a cheap and nasty bastard. Five percent is all he left for a tip." He pushed his chair back and slid out a keyboard drawer. He made a bunch of keystrokes, then slid the drawer back again. Phew. I figured he was ready for a break. He looked very serious when he said, "I hope you catch him, Mr. Dancer."

I paid him the hundred and he handed me the receipt. It was a Visa receipt in the amount of $24.75. He gave a token bow of his head and the hundred disappeared into his pocket. I stood up.

"A pleasure," I said.

"Give my regards to Clark, Mr. Dancer," he said.

"Clark?"

"Kent," he said.

Son of a gun.

He was a Superman fan after all.

Chapter Fifteen

DETECTING IS A FUNNY BUSINESS. We look for clues, little threads that lead us, we hope, to the next clue, always hoping to uncover the one big clue, through which a solution will transpire. The clue I currently held in my hand read "Oscar P. Wilson." The only Oscar P. Wilson in the Calgary phone book was a Reverend Oscar P. Wilson of the Baptist Revival Church on 14th Avenue in the northwest. An unlikely candidate for bank robbery but maybe the collection plate had been a little light of late. I parked in the parking lot and studied the building ahead of me. It was a nicely kept, cedar-sided, one-storey building with a fake steeple rising from the middle of the roof. Wide wooden steps led to the double front doors, one of which was held open by a chrome and brown leather chair.

I walked inside and felt the heat pressing down. The little church smelled stuffy, like there was a problem with the drains. Rows of pews to the left and right, a raised dais at the far end, a simple wooden cross affixed to the end wall. A black man in a white robe trimmed with bright crimson was working his way along the front row of pews, placing hymn books on the centre of each seat with great precision. I walked up the aisle towards him. He glanced up and smiled but continued placing the hymn books until he reached the end of the row. We stood facing each other, a few feet apart.

"Good morning." He spoke with a deep, cultured voice. "Isn't it a beautiful day?"

"Another beautiful day in Paradise," I agreed.

"Indeed it is. How may I help you?"

"Are you Oscar Wilson? The Reverend Oscar P. Wilson?"

"Yes?"

"You reported a missing credit card."

"I did?" He frowned. "No. I don't believe so. When was this?"

"A Visa card?"

"I have a Visa card. I don't believe it's missing." He withdrew a slim, black leather wallet from somewhere inside his robe. He peered inside. A narrow row of cards took up less than half of one side. Near the bottom, there was a gap. "Oh, dear."

"Oh dear?"

"I appear to be missing a card." He rifled through the wallet. "My Visa card. It is missing."

"No chance you left it somewhere by mistake? Like Ralph's Place last Friday?"

"Ralph's Place? I don't believe I know a Ralph's Place."

"It's a restaurant on Seventh Avenue. Downtown," I added, helpfully.

He shook his head.

"I rarely go downtown," he said. "This is a worry."

"Is this your signature, Reverend?" I pulled out the Visa receipt and handed it to him.

He studied it for a moment before shaking his head but his eyes gave him away.

"No. This is not my signature."

"You're sure?"

He nodded his head but would not meet my eye.

"But you know whose signature it is?" I quizzed him.

"Who are you, sir?" he asked.

"Eddie Dancer, Reverend. I'm a private detective."

I waited for his reaction but he remained steadfast and true. He gave me back the receipt.

"This is unofficial," I told him. "For now."

"Meaning?"

"Meaning it's unofficial if you tell me whose signature this is."

He shrugged.

"I couldn't be sure," he said.

"But you're sure it's not yours?"

"I'm sure."

"But you do recognize it?"

He bit his lip, then nodded.

"It's my brother's signature," he confessed. "He must have borrowed my card. He was here last week. Thursday."

"Where might I find him? Your brother?"

"In prison. He's serving a ten-year sentence for armed robbery."

"But he came to see you last Thursday?"

"Yes."

"Didn't you think that a bit odd?"

"No. He drops in from time to time."

"He's on day release?"

"I'm really not sure."

"When he comes to see you, is he handcuffed to a guard?"

"No."

"Never?"

"Never."

"He comes here unescorted?"

"Yes."

"But he's in prison for armed robbery?"

"Yes."

"Doing a ten-year stretch?"

"Yes. He's got six years left."

I was flummoxed.

"So where is he? When he's not enjoying some retail rehabilitation therapy with your credit card? Which prison?"

"He's an inmate of the Barbary Federal Prison."

"Are you expecting him again, sometime soon?"

"No. Maybe. Like I said, he just shows up."

"What's his name?"

The Reverend Oscar P. Wilson considered me for a moment.

"Phillip P. Wilson," he said, then. "Are you a God-fearing man, Edward?"

Edward.

It was the name my mother called me. God rest her soul, she never once called me Eddie.

"You could say that." I nodded.

"Is my brother in trouble?"

More trouble than you'll ever know, Reverend.

"Perhaps."

"Are you looking to hurt him, Edward?"

"Not necessarily."

"I ask because, if you are, you should know something about my brother." He looked me in the eye. "He is a mean and nasty motherfucker who will stop at nothing to get his own way. When they locked him up, Edward, they made a big mistake."

"Which was?"

"They forgot to throw away the key."

Ah. Brotherly love.

I left the Reverend Oscar P. Wilson to his hymn books and his cross to bear.

Chapter Sixteen

BACK IN NINETEEN EIGHTY-EIGHT, the City of Calgary hosted the Winter Olympic Games. Eddie the Eagle made headlines. I lived in Toronto at the time. I'd just turned twenty and still lived with my parents. My father worked for the government, doing what, I'm not really sure. He had vacation time owing and he and my mother decided to fly to Calgary and take in the games. Someone pulled some strings and got them tickets to various events. The hotels were all full and they settled on a motel off McLeod Trail, well south of the city centre. They had been gone three days when I received a phone call late in the evening. It was from the Calgary Coroner's office. My parents had both been killed by a hit-and-run driver less than an hour before.

I flew in that night. I was met at the airport by Paul Amos and Wendy Newbury, two detectives assigned to the case.

The accident happened on a side street, a few hundred yards from their motel. We stood on the street at two in the morning. Their best-guess scenario was based on the

position of the bodies. My father's body had lain in the gut-
ter closest to where we stood. My mother's body had been
thrown thirty-five feet across the road. There was a concrete
median that divided the street and my mother's body had
been thrown to the far side of the median. There was still
blood on the snow. Lots of it. The scenario had them crossing the street around five o'clock that evening, heading for
an early supper on McLeod Trail. The motel clerk had given
them direction to a nearby restaurant just minutes before
they were killed. I was informed that they had died instantly,
if that was any consolation.

Of course, it was no consolation at all.

The police were doing all they could to find the culprit
but they feared the driver had joined the traffic on McLeod
Trail and had disappeared.

I spent the night in their motel room — room 121. I
was stunned, too shocked to take it all in. I moved around
the room like a zombie. I opened the closet, touched their
clothes, stared at my father's things in the bathroom — his
razor. He used real razor blades. The thought of ending my
own life sidled across my mind. I was an orphan, an only
child. I'd been close to both my parents and the thought of
living without them was almost too much to bear. I sat on the
bed. There was a night table on my father's side. He always
slept on the left, my mother on the right. I could smell his
cologne on the pillow. I opened the drawers. In the bottom
drawer, under a paperback book, lay his wallet.

They were going out for supper.

Without his wallet.

My father was old-fashioned. He would never let my

mother pay. Perhaps they weren't headed for the restaurant after all. Perhaps they were headed back to the motel room so my father could pick up his wallet. He sometimes forgot things. But what difference would it make? Well, for one thing, it suggested that the car that hit them was going in the opposite direction because they had already crossed the road. They were towards the motel. But the broken headlight glass the police had found was on the west side of the road. Suppose the driver was drunk? Suppose he missed the median and had driven down the wrong side of the road? That would explain why they had stepped into the street without seeing the car. I roused the night manager and borrowed a street map. If I was right, if the driver had been driving north, not south, where was he headed? If he had been driving north, he was headed into a residential area with very few exits. Three, to be exact. I reasoned the driver was headed home because the street where it happened wasn't a cut-through. Anyone driving down that street had to be going into the residential district. Paul Amos was off duty by then but he drove back to the motel to meet with me. He listened carefully and studied the map. Finally, he looked up at me in the dim motel room light.

"You wanna ride shotgun?"

We drove every street and came up empty. Around six in the morning, we drove the back lanes and that's when we found a Ford Granada parked suspiciously close to the right-hand wall of a garage. The garage door looked damaged, like it hadn't opened in years. Small mercies. I followed Paul Amos through the snow and saw, in the unwavering beam of his flashlight, the damage to the front end of the Granada.

There were streaks of reddish-brown smeared along the front fender and across the hood. Paul Amos moved around the side of the car, tight against the garage wall. His flashlight played on something bright against the windshield, trapped beneath the crumpled edge of the hood. Using a knife blade, he prized free a shiny piece of metal. He held it in his open palm.

I can still see it.

It was a motel room key.

With 121 stamped across it.

We stood frozen in time for several long seconds. I felt the blood rush to my head. I wanted to smash down the door and do irreparable damage to the person inside. Paul Amos pushed me back to his car. I blinked back hot tears while he called for backup. We sat, immobile, as shadows flitted across the snow. A heavily armed SWAT team in helmets and goggles and flak jackets moved like ghosts through the snow, heavy-duty rifles trained on the house. The sonic boom of a battering ram split the early morning air and men with guns poured into the house.

I watched them drag my parents' killer through the back door, handcuff him and drag him across the yard, into the waiting police cruiser. I glimpsed his face. Haggard, scared, confused. He was hung over. A man in his mid-thirties, his licence suspended for driving drunk two months earlier.

I decided to stay in Calgary. My parents had died there and I felt a stronger connection to them by staying put. We'd moved many times in the past and I had no real affinity to anywhere else. Paul Amos helped me. We became friends. He helped me again, two years later, when I applied for a job on the Calgary City Police Force. I was a cop for two years. I enjoyed it but I ran into problems with management. I have a teeny bit of a problem dealing with authority figures. I'm too much the smart-ass, too much the shortcut king. We parted ways on relatively good terms and Paul Amos and I have remained friends. I have other friends on the force. I couldn't do my job without them. Sometimes I scratch their back, sometimes they scratch mine.

Which is how I managed to cut through all the red tape and arranged to meet the elusive Phillip P. Wilson, serving a ten-year sentence for armed robbery in the Barbary Federal Prison.

Chapter Seventeen

I LOATHE THE SMELL OF PRISONS. They smell of fear and putrid food, of animals and wet pelts and fetid earth and urine and excrement. And the Barbary smells of something else. Something that rubs your nerve endings raw from the moment you walk in through the tall outer gate. The guards in the gatehouse stare at you with flat dead eyes behind mirrored sunglasses as you pass by. That other smell is the odour of unadulterated evil and you pray the men behind the mirrored sunglasses will let you out again.

I wasn't carrying my gun so the brooding metal detector beyond the tall inner gate remained silent and thwarted. A tall guard, with skull-cut hair, walked me down a long corridor that echoed and through steel doors that reverberated when he slammed them shut behind me. He sat me in a metal chair bolted to the floor of a long, narrow room made entirely of concrete. A half wall topped with thick, tempered glass, cross-hatched with chicken wire, separated me from the inmates. There was no one else in the visitors' room. Seven empty chairs. A door opened at the end of the corridor behind the glass. A big black man in prison blues shuffled in. He glared at me, not knowing who I was. He turned back to the door but it closed behind him so he turned back to glare at me some more. There was a family resemblance but I didn't think Phillip P. would look good in a dog collar and white robes.

"Phillip Wilson?"

"Who are you?"

"I want to talk to you."

"Fuck you. I don't know you. Get outta here."

I stayed put.

"I'm a friend of a friend."

"I don't got friends."

"Joe Baker."

He looked surprised, even scared. He looked around quickly like he was afraid of being overheard. He hurried towards me, his demeanour suddenly urgent, clearly disturbed by my presence. He sat behind the glass, his face pressed close to mine.

"Are you crazy?" he hissed. "You wanna get us whacked? Get the fuck outta here! Don't you ever come back, you hear?"

"And Dick Wyman says to say hello."

His shoulders slumped. His face looked ravaged.

"You want to talk to me, Phillip, or you want to tell me to fuck off again?"

"You have any idea what you messing with?"

"Tell me."

"Fuck you." He banged his fists hard against the chicken-wired glass. "Get the fuck outta here while you still got two good legs."

He pushed himself away from the glass and stood up. He wiped his nose on his sleeve then walked back to the door at the far end of the corridor.

"Two-Seven-Eight-Four-Nine-Two-Six requests permission to go back to his cell! Sir!"

The door opened and Phillip P. Wilson, Prisoner Two-Seven-Eight-Four-Nine-Two-Six, never even looked back.

And I walked away on my two good legs.

Chapter Eighteen

I DROVE BACK TO THE CITY with the windows down but even that failed to wash the stench of the Barbary from my skin. I'd found the elusive mastermind but, in finding him, I'd uncovered more questions than answers. Like how did he get to be in two places at once? And what was he afraid of? I cruised slowly past my office, drove around the block, parked on the street and left the Blazer's doors unlocked. Once inside the hall, I stayed close to the wall, passed the painters' equipment, passed The Kid in his studio. He had his back to me, headphones over his ears, fingers flying over the keyboard.

But something was wrong.

My door.

The shadow along the doorjamb was too wide. I moved closer. The door wasn't closed tightly. Close up, I saw the door lock had been jimmied. I pressed my ear against the door and listened. I could hear the sounds of the building, like a living animal. I wished I'd worn my gun.

I pushed the door open with my foot and almost rolled

across the floor the way real detectives do on television. I'm glad I didn't. I would have come to a sticky end. Someone had poured a half a dozen gallons of paint all over my office. Wedgwood Green over my desk and filing cabinet and Desert Mocha over the chairs and carpet. The effect was even more horrible because they hadn't mixed the paint so it ran in streaks with base white fanning out from the middle.

If there was any doubt who had done it, the answer was on the wall. In Wedgwood Green paint, with a four-inch brush, they had written "DICK THIS MOTHERFUCKER." I guess I had that coming. I decided against using my office phone. It was covered in sticky wet paint. I called 411 on my cell phone and asked for the number for WeCleanAll. A nice lady called Marjorie tut-tutted and said they could have Brian, their estimator, pop round later that day. I said I'd leave the door unlocked and to be sure to tell Brian to wear his wellies.

That's Nosher and Splosher talk for big rubber booties.

I returned several phone calls on my voice mail, turning down yet another job. The last message was from Nurse Nightingale. Cindy. She said Angie's condition had stabilized but there had been no other improvement. She also said she'd been digging through the medical records and had come up with something curious and to please call her. She left her home phone number.

I didn't need to be told twice.

I called her back right away but got her answering machine. It said her name was Cindy Palmer and to please leave a message. I left a message then tried her at the hospital but they said she was off for the next two days.

I needed a plan. It's what detectives are supposed to do. Discover clues and make plans to get the bad guys.

Having trashed my office, I figured Len and Doug were probably less of a threat now, but I couldn't rule them out of my life just yet. And then there was Phillip P. Wilson who seemed to have a "get out of jail free" card whenever he needed one. Just who was he afraid of? And should I be afraid of them too? And who the hell were they?

I decided it was time to cover my butt. I phoned my pickup guy, Danny Many Guns.

I first met Danny in a bar on Electric Avenue, when Electric Avenue was the place to be seen if you were under thirty. It's all changed now, of course, but ten years ago it was hopping. The bar was almost empty that early in the afternoon, the day crowd still recovering from the night before. I'd stopped by for a cold beer. Danny Many Guns, a full-blooded North American Indian, was standing at the bar, drinking something that looked suspiciously like lemonade. He stood tall and slim in a two-piece, dark blue suit with a light blue shirt and a deep red power tie. Jet-black hair swept back from his forehead, high cheekbones and perfectly even, white-on-white teeth — a good-looking dude. He could have been a native American movie star. Until he looked you in the eye. Then he looked downright scary. He had one very dark brown eye and one very pale grey eye. You wanted to look away and yet you didn't. The pale grey eye stabbed you like a laser beam.

I stood five feet to his right and leaned on the bar, watching the reflection of the two cowboy wannabes who tripped coming into the bar. They were both well oiled with necks red enough to stop traffic. "All balls and biceps," as Nosher might say. The first guy lurched as he crossed behind Danny Many Guns, spilling beer down the back of Danny's beautiful suit. He made a comment about clumsy Indians and put his beer glass down on an empty table. He walked back to Danny Many Guns and accused him of spilling his beer. I watched the barman continue to polish the glasses. He didn't seem unduly concerned for Danny Many Guns' safety. Maybe he didn't give a damn. Or maybe he knew something about Danny Many Guns that I didn't.

Danny turned to face the redneck cowboy wannabe and the effect of the pale grey eye backed the guy up a couple of feet.

"I beg your pardon?" Danny spoke so softly, you'd strain to hear him.

"Are you fuckin' deaf?" The redneck moved back in Danny's face.

"No." Danny moved his head left to right.

The cowboy wannabe put his right hand flat on Danny's chest and tried to push him over the bar but as he did so, Danny placed both of his hands over the top of the cowboy's, trapping them against his chest. Then he simply dropped to the floor as if he was going to squat a great weight. It was a fast and simple move and you could hear the wannabe's wrist break clear across the room. He screamed as he rolled across the floor and the second wannabe pulled a blade. I'd moved six inches to take it off him when Danny Many Guns hit him upside the head, a spin-kick with the power of a mule's hind leg. The guy never knew what hit him. He was out cold on the barroom floor.

I turned the six inches back to the bar.

The barman never missed a beat, just kept wiping the glasses and stacking them behind the bar. Danny Many Guns shot his cuffs, turned back to the bar and took another sip of his lemonade.

"Thank you," he said without turning his head but I knew he was talking to me.

"For what?"

"Being my pickup guy."

"You didn't need one."

"It was the thought that counted."

"Then you're welcome."

The barman slid a cold beer in front of me. He inclined his head slightly, a gift from the Indian. We clinked glasses, falling into an easy conversation. I'm not a person who needs well-wishers or fair-weather friends. I believe, by the time you die, if you can count your friends on the fingers of one hand, you've done well. Danny Many Guns and I became friends after that first meeting. Though I know him well, he still remains an enigma. He always will. It's a cultural thing, I guess, but I'm not hung up on understanding his every thought. We might not see one another for weeks, even months, but when we do, it's like nothing has changed. We pick up the beat without missing a cue. Danny is a Harvard business graduate. He made his fortune playing the stock market.

"Dot-com stock," he once told me. "I knew the bubble would burst pretty quickly, but I still had time to invest."

He once told me how much he'd made in dot-com days. To make that sort of money, I'd need to buy a lottery ticket.

Now, he ran his own company and represented gifted Indian artists. Truly talented ones whose work, with Danny's help, reached a very wealthy and appreciative audience.

"Where'd you learn to kick like that?" I asked.

"I went to a mixed school," he said. "Me and six hundred white kids. My father got tired of dressing my wounds. He took me to see some of our people — ancient warriors. I spent an entire summer with them. They taught me many things."

Later that summer, Danny taught me those things the warriors had taught him. And in return, I taught Danny a few wrinkles of my own.

I called him on my cell phone.

"Wigwam Exports."

That's Indian humour.

I told him my problem, offered him a pittance to protect my ass then halved it when he squawked.

I'd barely hung up when my cell phone rang again. I checked the number.

Heavens to Betsy.

Nurse Nightingale.

"Still want to buy me that coffee?" she said.

"Mochaccino?"

"Decaf, black, no sugar."

"Tell me where you live, I'll deliver."

She gave me her address. "Two blocks west of the new Starbucks," she said.

How cool was that?

Chapter Nineteen

I WAS ABOUT TO RING THE BELL when I was almost creamed by a young lady, maybe ten or eleven years of age. She was just leaving as I arrived and she almost barrelled into me as she flung the door open wide and came charging out.

"Oops! Sorry! Mom!" she yelled over her shoulder, rolling all her words into one. "Somebody here!" then disappeared down the walkway in a cloud of dust.

Nurse Nightingale lived otherwise alone with a lady cat oddly named Norman, who was too affectionate for her own good. She climbed all over me and dipped her tail in my coffee.

The cat did.

Nurse Nightingale, or more correctly, Cindy Palmer, lived in a stylish townhouse complex with lots of trees and front verandas. There were footpaths from the visitors' parking lot that wound around the trees, making room for Mother Nature. I liked that. A nice touch. The whole place had a well-kept quality. It wasn't gated but it looked relaxed and appealing. So did Cindy Palmer in tight blue jeans with a white halter top. I'm not sure what a halter top really is but it lay across her breasts in a pleasing manner and offered a tantalizing glimpse of her midriff when she reached up so it was a halter top by my definition.

Though it wouldn't offer much haltering, given half a chance.

"What did you find?" I asked, once I got settled in.

We were sitting in her family room. Cream-coloured leather Lay-Z-Boys, a big-screen TV and a polished oak coffee table. The lady had great taste. She sipped her decaf then placed it carefully on the coaster of a cat curled in a basket. Cat art dotted the walls and peeked out from amid the shelving. A pair of plaid-coloured stuffed cats hung from the tops of the hi-fi speakers and when Cindy Palmer curled up in the armchair across from me, she even resembled a cat.

"You could be right about Angie," she began. "Toxicology didn't find any drugs in her bloodstream. Nothing. Doesn't mean she hasn't taken any but it's doubtful drugs were the cause of the problem."

"I feel vindicated," I said, "though none the wiser."

"I got thinking about the other girls." She picked up her coffee, her eyes watching me just above the rim.

"What other girls?"

"The others that came through Emerge. Brain-fried vegetables."

She made them sound like a side dish.

"Yes. I remember you said something about them. One or two a month."

She sipped her coffee, both hands wrapped around the mug as though she were cold.

"I searched the records. Over the past two years, we've seen seventeen girls with identical symptoms. I called Foothills Hospital and they've seen about twelve in the same time period."

"Nothing before that?"

"No." She shook her head and took another sip of coffee. "Twenty-nine girls," she said. "Only three were decisive."

"Does that mean functional?"

"Barely. They didn't defecate the bed. But the remaining twenty-six were virtually brain dead. They couldn't speak, no visual recognition, no thought processes. They were vegetables."

"All hookers?"

"As far as we could tell."

"Twenty-nine of them?"

She nodded, watching me over the rim.

"Do you want the printouts?" she asked.

"Their medical records?"

She shook her head. "Those are private. I mean the stat printouts. No names, just the time and place, the attending doctor and such." She sipped her coffee. She was watching me like a hawk.

"You won't get in trouble?"

She shrugged.

"Have you talked to anyone else about this?"

"Everyone's too busy coping with the bed shortage. They haven't the manpower to start an investigation."

"That's too bad." I watched her some more. "So you want me to have the records?"

"If you think they'll help."

"This case I'm working on." I sipped from my own cup.
"It doesn't involve Angie."

"Doesn't it?" Her chin came up, a defensive posture full
of challenge.

"Not directly." I took another sip. We were watching
each other over the rims of our cups, playing out the string.
"But if I stumbled on a connection, be nice to have some
backup material."

"And if you find a connection?" she asked.

I shrugged. "I'll disconnect it," I said.

"Promise?"

She watched me, her eyes unblinking.

"Twenty-nine people," I said, "seems like a lot."

"It's a goddamned epidemic," she said and her eyes
flashed. She was taking this personally.

"You have the printouts?"

"No, but I can run them off for you."

"You can do it from here?"

She gave me a look, unfurled her legs and padded across
the room.

"Come on."

I followed her upstairs. Her hips took on a delicious roll
and her derriere was a delight. Be still my beating heart. She
turned into a bedroom set up like an office. A computer
monitor sat on the desktop. Her screen saver was a picture
of herself in a bikini, water-skiing across a blue lake. I leaned
in for a closer look but the picture changed. Now she was
standing near the top of a mountain and jeans and a long
wool sweater had replaced the bikini. Crap! She nudged the
mouse and the Windows screen popped up.

"Grab a seat."

I let that pass and grabbed a chair instead. It took her maybe ten minutes to access the information.

"My printer's been acting up," she said, looking back over her shoulder. "This could take a while."

"That's fine," I said.

"Have you had lunch?"

I shook my head.

We sat in the kitchen and, as I watched her build me a ham and cheese sandwich on rye bread, I questioned her gently about her past.

"I was married once — once was enough." She smiled when she said it so I guessed things went sour a while back. "You?"

I shook my head. "Never met the right girl, I guess." Though I thought I had on a few occasions, until my commitment gene kicked into overdrive and left me alone and unattached.

"It wasn't a bad divorce. As divorces go. Lindsay still sees her dad once or twice a month. He's a cop."

What is it with nurses and cops? Maybe they both have the same warped sense of humour.

"Lindsay's your daughter?"

"Yes."

"She has your eyes," I said. "Have you talked to your ex about this?"

"About the girls?" She licked a dab of mayo off her fingers. "No. He's a traffic cop. Besides, I already told you, we don't have the manpower to become involved in an investigation. Patient care would suffer."

She sprinkled brown sugar on mustard, mixed them together and spread a slab on the ham.

"You're planning on eating that one, are you?" I said.

"Half," she said. "Don't worry about the brown sugar. It's an old Russian recipe. It makes the mustard taste better. Trust me. I'm a nurse."

I watched her. She had small hands and sensitive fingers that moved with minimum fuss, a delicate economy suggesting a busy life.

"Have you always been a nurse?"

"No. I used to be a toddler, then a teenager, then a nurse." She cut the double-decker firmly in half.

Funny girl.

"Must be hectic. E.R. and all."

"Yes. I used to be a geriatric nurse but I couldn't hack it. I worked in a seniors' lodge. Same old, same old, then they die. Very hard to take. Now, every day is different." She handed me a plate. "Here you go." The rye bread sandwich was stacked thick with ham and cheese. "Or would you like to eat outside?"

She stood up and I followed her out onto her deck. The fenced yard was small and full of shrubs and flowers. I was surprised how much privacy she had. Built into the far end of the deck was a six-person hot tub. The lid was closed but wisps of steam escaped the edges.

"Am I interrupting something?" I nodded at the tub but she shook her head.

"No. I'll probably have a soak later."

I tried to imagine that but it was too distracting. I concentrated on the sandwich instead.

"So." She spoke around a cheek full of ham. "How's the sandwich?"

It was good. Surprisingly good. The sugar added a delicate flavour to the ham and cheese. She seemed pleased when I told her I really liked it.

"Next time, lunch is on me," I told her.

"You think there'll be a next time?"

"That's entirely up to you."

"I was thinking dinner."

Damn.

I was thinking breakfast.

We sat and talked, basking in the shade and enjoying the warmth that spread between us. Norman, the lady cat, appeared and wrapped herself around my legs, then, uninvited but not unwelcome, she hopped onto my lap and nuzzled the top of her head against the underside of my chin. She purred loudly.

"Put her down if she's bothering you," Cindy said.

"She's not."

When the head butting ended, Norman made herself comfortable in my lap. She walked in little circles before deciding on the most comfortable spot, flopped over and fell asleep with all four legs sticking straight out.

"You like cats?" Cindy asked.

"Sure. I like most animals."

"We had a cat at the seniors' lodge. A Russian Blue."

I frowned — I wouldn't know a Russian Blue from a Polynesian Pink.

"They're grey," she said. "With green eyes."

"Okay." I nodded. I'd seen grey cats before.

"We named her Lucky. When someone got really sick, she used to go lie on their bed. Wouldn't move, just lay there until they passed on. Like she knew. Happened every time."

"Maybe she was secretly killing them," I said. "Death by giant hairball."

She glanced over at me, her mouth in a half-smile. "Oh," she said, "you'll get yours."

We sat quietly for a time, until Norman let out a very unladylike snore that made us both giggle.

"That's a good sign," Cindy told me. "Means she trusts you. Snoring means she's very relaxed."

"So." I stepped up to the plate. "Do you snore?"

"I don't know." She looked grave. "It's been a long time . . ." She let the sentence hang. Perhaps she regretted it.

"Must be tough, having a daughter."

"Tougher than you think."

"Let me guess. You run suitable candidates by the ex before you date them?"

She didn't look surprised.

"You have no idea how many weirdos there are out there," she said.

"Maybe the ex is a little jealous? Feeds you back a little dirt?"

"He remarried. Nothing would make him happier than to see me in the same position, believe me."

"So how come we're doing this?" I indicated the food, the table, the picnic outdoors. "Haven't got round to checking me out yet?"

"I checked you out." She grinned, a quick, mischievous smirk. "You're one of the good guys."

"I try to be," I told her, "I surely do."

After lunch, she cleaned off the table. She was gone a few minutes and when she returned, she was carrying a stack of paper from the printer. I'd almost forgotten why I was there. She handed the papers to me.

I scanned the reports. They all said basically the same thing. Each patient was identified by age and by sex. The doctor's name and the date appeared at the bottom. I turned back a page. The attending doctor had added something to one case.

"What does *'syndrome du bébé securé'* mean?"

My French wasn't good. Actually, it was lousy.

"Show me."

I gave her the sheet.

"Don't know." She shook her head. "That's Doctor LaRue. He's French. He does that sometimes, adds a little Français."

"Can you ask him?"

"Sure." She stood up. "I'll see if he's working."

She went back into the kitchen and I heard her talking on the phone, then a few minutes of silence, followed by more talking before she hung up. She came back on the deck.

"It means Shaken Baby Syndrome," she said and as she said it, I felt something, something chilly and cold, slither down my spine.

For a moment, I was transported somewhere else. First, my office in the city where cans of unmixed paint stained the carpet. Then to a garage in the darkness where I barked my shin on something made of metal. Something bolted to the floor.

"Are you okay?"

"I'm not sure," I said.

"You look like you've seen a ghost."

"Maybe I have. Listen, can I take these?"

I touched the sheets and she nodded. I rolled them up and tucked them in my pocket.

"I have to go."

She looked surprised. I stood up. She stood up directly in front of me.

"Are you okay?" Concerned.

"I'm sure it's nothing," I lied. "I just need to check something out."

"Okay." She inclined her head to one side. "Stop by sometime," she said and put her hand on my arm.

Maybe she was just feeling my pulse.

"Thanks again for lunch. And thanks for your help with Angie." I turned to go. "I'll call you."

"That's what they all say."

At the door, she laid her hand on my arm again.

"Eddie, be careful," she said.

It was an odd yet strangely prophetic thing to say.

I blew her a kiss as I hurried back to the Blazer.

Chapter Twenty

I SAT WITH DANNY MANY GUNS in his downtown high-rise office. Rich mahogany desk and credenza, burgundy leather chesterfields, glass-topped coffee table and a wall of backlit glass shelving, a display area for the very expensive, high-end Indian art he sold. No cotton dream catchers here, no moccasins or bead necklaces. Danny only dealt in the real stuff. Hand-carved soapstone was the item of the day.

"You broke into their place?" he said.

"Yes."

"Without backup?"

Meaning without him.

"Yes. I was in and out real quick."

He looked at me. His one grey eye spoke volumes.

"And what did you see?"

"I didn't see it. I whacked my shin on it. It was bolted to the floor."

"Tell me again what it was."

"A paint mixer."

He frowned.

"A paint shaker, then. You still see them in old hardware stores. Half-horse motor attached to circular metal plates on big springs. You drop the paint can between the plates, tighten them up, turn it on. It vibrates the paint for a minute, maybe two and then the paint in the can's all mixed."

"And you think they put your friend Angie in this paint mixer?"

"Yes. It's big enough to put someone's head in. Tighten up the plates, turn it on. Maybe ten seconds, maybe half a minute, I don't know. The impact on the brain would be devastating."

"And the others?"

"I don't know."

"But you think your friend isn't the first?"

"Yes."

"What do you want to do about it?"

"Shake them up."

"I think you already have."

"Put them out of business. Permanently."

"You could call the police," he said, like he really believed that was an option.

"I have no evidence."

"I see."

He was silent for a while. Before either of us spoke again, my cell phone rang. I glanced at the number. It was Nosher.

"Hello?"

"You know a bird named Velvet?" Nosher said.

"Yes."

"Thought so. She's here. An' she's 'urt." There was a hard edge to his voice.

"How bad?"

"Bad. Some arsehole has beaten her with a wire coat hanger. A red 'ot one."

"I'm on the way."

I hung up. Danny was already on his feet.

"I'll drive," he said.

I didn't argue. I was preoccupied with a feeling that things were just beginning to spin out of control.

Chapter Twenty-One

THIS MONTH, ĐANNY WAS DRIVING a yellow Hummer. I rappelled into the passenger seat and stared down on the sunroofs of almost every other car on the road. He wheeled expertly through the traffic, never wasting space to make a lane change. He knew exactly how hard the tires would squeal before losing traction and he drove on that edge. We got to the acreage in record time.

"Who's Hot Wheels?" Nosher asked as he met us at the front door.

"Her pimp," I told him and his face got hard but he didn't say anything else.

Velvet was lying face down on Nosher's bed. They had given her Percocet for the pain but she wanted something stronger. They had covered her with a clean, fresh sheet but she had pulled it off. Her back and buttocks were cross-hatched with brutally thin burn lines that cut deep into her flesh. I counted maybe twenty separate strokes. The pain must have been intolerable.

I sat down carefully next to her. She moaned and turned

her head. Her eyes were wild with anger.

"This is all your fault," she hissed at me.

"I didn't whip you, Velvet."

"He knew we took Angie to the hospital." Her breathing was short and fast.

"He did this because you cared about your friend?"

"No. Because I went with you."

"You went with Angie. She was your friend."

"Not anymore."

"I'm still your friend, Velvet." I let that hang for a moment. "You need a doctor."

"I need a fix."

"Let me take you to the hospital."

"No."

I waited but that was all she said.

"They'll help you," I told her.

"They'll call the cops."

"And that's a bad thing?"

"Yeah." She winced as she moved her hair from her shoulders.

"You think he'll take you back?"

"I dunno."

"I do."

"It hurts real bad."

"I know. Let me take you to Emergency." I wondered if Cindy would be there.

"No."

The air in the room stirred. I glanced back. Danny was standing behind me. He looked down at the long red lines of abused flesh.

"Can you stand?" he asked her gently.

She looked up at him and shrugged. "I guess."

He took the crumpled bed sheet. With a small, sharp knife, he cut a hole in the centre and fashioned a top for her. With his help, she stood up and I maintained a sense of modesty by keeping her covered with a fresh sheet. Danny guided her head through the hole in the sheet, then tied it off around the back of her neck. It covered her front but lay open around the back so it wouldn't rub against her burns.

"There's a sweat lodge about an hour from here," Danny said to me. "Some people I know will help her through this."

We helped Velvet down to the Hummer. We lay her across the back seat and thanked Nosher and his brother for their help. They didn't say anything but a look passed between them and I knew they were planning Velvet's revenge. I hoped they would include me. I climbed in beside Danny and he drove gently back down the long drive.

About a year after I met him, Danny took me running. Not the sort of run I expected. We went out in the bush, running across open country, fording rivers, running hard up hills, running harder down the far side. We ran through thick forests and open fields of wildflowers. After the first hour, I thought I was going to be sick but Danny urged me on. I got my second wind. After another hour, I threw up. Danny said that was a good sign. We kept running. After three and a half hours I hit the wall. Somehow, my legs stayed the course but my brain gave out. It left me. I'm not talking about a runner's high. This went way beyond that, way beyond anything I'd experienced in my entire life. We ran for six hours, stopping only to drink from ice-water streams. I wore a pair of one hundred and forty dollar Nikes, Danny wore a pair of handmade moccasins. I ran in such pain, I thought I would pass out. Danny told me not to see the pain as something separate but to embrace it — to be at one with it. I watched him run. He seemed to function beyond the pain, to override it, somehow. And then, slowly, mile by mile, I began to understand and, eventually, I passed right through the pain and I, too, moved beyond it, to a higher plane. It was the most spiritual experience I've ever had. And it's very comforting to know that there is a place you can reach that is above and beyond whatever pain you can endure.

Near the end of the run, he ripped his T-shirt on a broken tree branch and I saw an unpleasant, puckered scar on his chest. When I asked about it later, he took off the T-shirt and showed me twin scars, ugly knots that ran deep into both of his pectoral muscles. As a teenager, he'd been expected to spend the night in a kind of sweat lodge. It was a shelter built of branches and hung with brightly coloured cloth. Inside, two sharpened hooks, attached to chains, hung from a pole high in the ceiling. It was a rite of passage from childhood to manhood. He smoked sweet grass to help endure the excruciating pain. The elders pushed the sharpened hooks into the pectoral muscles as though they were baiting a fishing line. They raised him up on chains and left him hanging from the roof pole. He told me it took him almost two hours. His pectoral muscles were strong and thick and heavy as marine rope. He kicked and writhed, twisting his body against the hard steel of the hooks set deep in his chest. Blood slicked his entire body. He rested, each time for longer periods, while the elders encouraged him and gave him more sweet grass to inhale.

Finally, the last of the tendrils of flesh and muscle gave way and he crashed to the ground. They tended his wounds and laid him out on a cot where he stayed for almost a week until the blood stopped flowing and the scars on his chest began to form.

After that, he made a promise never to permit such a thing again. He worked to change the very nature of the sweat lodge, to bring it back as a place of healing, a place of cleansing, and never again a rite of passage. At first, there was much opposition but he persevered until, eventually, reason won and his people agreed to work with him.

The sweat lodge where we took Velvet was a healing place. The elders spoke softly, mixing herbs and roots and ancient remedies they said would quash her pain, heal her scars. They poured water over hot stones to produce a heavy steam and they guided smoke from burning sweet grass across her ravaged body and into her lungs. We were invited to stay the night and slept in narrow cots a few inches off the ground. Danny fell asleep almost immediately but I lay awake for hours, sweating in the moist heat and staring at the ceiling, cross-hatched with thick branches, and I imagined strong young men writhing on chains until their bodies split open and they fell, bleeding, to the floor.

In the morning, we rose early. Velvet seemed rested and much of the pain had left her but the healing had a long way to go. We wished her well and drove back to the city. I picked up my Blazer from Danny Many Guns' office and he told me he would be watching my back.

I was sure glad someone was.

Chapter Twenty-Two

IT WAS MIDMORNING BY THE TIME I ARRIVED at my office. WeCleanAll had already started. The furniture had been moved, the carpet ripped out and a huge industrial heater was drying the last of the paint on the walls. Two men in one-piece overalls were sweating hard, cleaning up the last of the damage.

"Your place?" one of them yelled above the racket of the heater.

"Yeah!"

"It'll take us most of the day!"

"Take as long as you need!" I yelled back.

"The locksmith's on his way!"

"Tell him to leave the keys next door!" I waved towards The Kid's studio.

The temperature was unbearable. Even hotter than the sweat lodge. When I stepped back outside, my shirt stuck to my skin. Time to head home for a shower and a change of clothes. I circled the block looking for signs of unrest and Harley motorcycles but saw nothing out of the ordinary. My house is a small two storey, an older home on a quiet street of similar homes. Pride of ownership in abundance. Most homeowners had repainted the cedar exterior but one or two had replaced it with vinyl. We had discussed voting them off the street or burning them at the stake but never got around to it. I had bought the place the year after my parents died. My father carried life insurance and both my parents had made out their wills a few years before they died. As their only child, I received a lump sum settlement, more than enough to buy the house outright. I liked the area and felt it would appreciate in value over the coming years, so I spent the next twelve months fixing it up. I removed walls, installed high-tensile beams, ripped out carpets and lino and I replaced it with gleaming hardwood. I installed maple cabinetry in the kitchen with an island and breakfast bar. The back garden was my favourite place to sit and contemplate nature. I had seventeen mature trees and I'd built an irregular shaped deck that encompassed eight of them. I hung brightly coloured hammocks between their stout trunks, built a brick barbecue, tore down the rickety fence and replaced it with a six-foot solid structure that did nothing to keep out the squirrels. If I forgot to close the patio door, the squirrels would come in, climb on the kitchen counter and raid the cookie jar.

The bathroom was huge. I'd knocked out the adjoining wall and expanded it into the third bedroom. The shower was the focal point. More than enough room for two, it had four chrome bars, one in each corner with adjustable showerheads that moved up and down the bars. Hit four ways with pulsating jets of hot water, you came out feeling reborn.

I towelled off and found a clean shirt in my wardrobe. A pair of blue jeans hung from the corner bedpost. I grabbed them just as the doorbell rang. The master bedroom faces front. I saw the Cockney twins' tow truck outside on the street and went downstairs to let them in.

"Hey-up," Splosher said. "Got a mo'?"

"Sure. You wanna come in?"

"Nah." It was Nosher's turn. "Come for a ride."

I grabbed a pair of sandals and followed them back to the truck. The three of us sat across the worn front seat.

"Where are we going?"

"You'll see."

Splosher drove. I had no idea where we were going but I had a good idea what might be involved. He pulled the truck into a narrow residential street across from a two-storey wooden apartment building, parking a few doors down from a black Cadillac convertible.

I might have guessed.

Nosher left the engine running with the air conditioning on. It was after one o'clock when we arrived and we waited almost an hour in the hot afternoon sun. I would have dozed off but something was digging in my hip and I was too polite to wake up Splosher so I could make myself more comfortable. Then Nosher nudged me in the ribs.

"Hey-up," he said. "Here he comes."

Hot Wheels stepped out of the apartment building and headed across the street towards his car. He looked like he'd just got up. Ah, the life of a pimp. Party all night, sleep away half the day. He fished his keys from his pocket, unlocked the door and slid behind the wheel of the huge Caddy. Nosher switched off the engine and wound down the window, the better to hear what was coming.

Hot Wheels cranked the ignition and the Caddy made a horrible grinding sound before the engine caught and held. Hot Wheels revved it in disbelief. It didn't sound like a Cadillac at all.

"What the hell?" I looked from one to the other. "What have you done?"

"What's it sound like?" Nosher said.

I listened some more. It didn't sound like anything I'd heard before, certainly nothing like a Cadillac should.

Then I got it.

"It's a Volkswagen," I said. "You pulled the motor?"

"Last night. He's got a nineteen seventy-four Volkswagen Beetle motor with a couple hundred thou on the clock," Nosher said proudly.

Hot Wheels popped the hood and stepped out.

"Stay here," Splosher said. "This one's on us."

They climbed from the truck and walked towards Hot Wheel as he lifted the hood.

Nosher came up alongside him and Splosher came around the far side. They stood close. Suddenly, Hot Wheels moved back, but he wasn't fast enough. Splosher's curled fist hit him hard in the kidneys and doubled him up. They grabbed him, an arm and a leg apiece, and quickly stuffed him, head first, inside the now-more-roomy engine compartment of the Cadillac. Then they slammed the hood. It had taken less than ten seconds. They looked around. Nobody was watching. Nobody cared. They walked back to the tow truck.

"Payback," Nosher said, "is a beautiful thing."

We drove sedately past the Caddy. The engine was still running.

"You're going to leave him there?"

"Sure," Nosher confirmed. "There's room. Sort of. We left out the radiator."

"And sharpened the fan blades," Splosher said.

I thought about that and I wondered how long it would take for the engine to get really hot. And I thought about Hot Wheels, jammed in a tight, dark, noisy space, upside down, just inches from a razor sharp, high-speed fan.

"Oh yeah," Nosher said, remembering something. "And we put a few extra gallons in his gas tank, make sure he doesn't run out of gas."

"Jesus," I said. "Remind me never to piss you guys off."

They had a good laugh at that.

Chapter Twenty-Three

THE COCKNEY TWINS DROPPED ME back home and I used the rest of the day to catch up on business. I reflected on Hot Wheels' predicament. The plight of Angie and the sight of Velvet justified whatever hell he was going through. I put him out of my mind. I returned outstanding phone calls, paid a bunch of bills and finally figured out what had been digging in my hip. It was the half dozen metal VIN tags I'd taken from Len and Doug's garage. I spread them across the kitchen counter and copied down the numbers on a clean sheet of paper, tucking it away in the back of my wallet. Officially, I was still working for Dick and Sue-Ann Wyman. Although the investigation had detoured through Len and Doug and ultimately to Hot Wheels, my focus was still on finding out what I could about Phillip P. Wilson. But I still needed to protect my butt where Len and Doug were concerned. I needed a little leverage.

It was time to head back downtown.

The parking garage on 6th was full so I parked at a meter. I took a parking ticket from my glove box and tucked it under the windshield wiper. The parking authority was not allowed to put more than one ticket on your windshield at any one time.

At Police Headquarters, I took the elevator to the sixth floor.

Dana Parker looked ravishing as ever. We'd dated a few times and I know she's one of the very few true redheads left on the planet. Dana and I had become friends when I was a city cop. Now, she ran an entire police department and looked harried, standing with a phone jammed under her chin. I tapped on her door and admired her legs.

"Go away, I'm busy," she said when she saw me.

"Is this the Lost and Found?"

"I mean it." She glanced at me, her green eyes not missing a thing. "Leave that —" she jabbed a well-manicured finger toward the sheet of paper I had taken from my wallet "— there —" pointing to the corner of her desk. She turned her back on me.

I borrowed her pen and wrote my fax number on the sheet. She'd know what to do. It wasn't the first time I'd asked.

"Can you fix a parking ticket?" I said as I was leaving.

She didn't even turn around, just floated her index finger in my direction.

Like most men, I hate to shop. It was close to suppertime but I needed to replace the things that Len and Doug had wrecked. I picked up a new fax machine at Office Depot and loaded up with coloured file folders and matching hanging files. I added matching pen sets, a matching desk pad, a matching diary, matching paperclips and matching push pins for the corkboard. I went with a plain beige desk phone, the cordless model so I could talk on the can.

By seven-thirty, I was exhausted. I drove home, circled the block twice looking for nonexistent spies, left everything in the Blazer and went inside to raid the fridge. The choice was beer or Coke for supper. Not much of a raid. I took the beer. I like dark beer that bites back. Dark beer with a thick blonde head.

I drank three of them before I remembered my fridge was empty of food. It was too far, and too hot, to walk to the store and, after three beers, I wasn't about to drive.

So I had a liquid supper. Three more beers and by ten o'clock I was too pooped to party. I fell into bed as the room began to spin. Snoring never came easier. I wondered if Cindy Palmer snored.

Norman snores.

Funny name for a cat.

Especially a lady cat.

I awoke around two to a sound far worse than my snoring. It was a metallic sound, the unmistakable sound of someone putting a bullet under the hammer. A kind of snick-click sound magnified a thousand-fold in a bedroom with hardwood floors. It was a sound that set my nerves on edge, tightening my muscles to excruciating tension and holding the breath in my lungs until I thought I was going to explode. But it cleared my head real fast. I remembered to breathe. It was important to make the gunman think I was still asleep, all the while slowly moving my legs towards the edge of the bed.

Christ, why did I own a king-sized bed? I was lost amid

a Siberia of linen that stretched to an impossible horizon. I sidled towards the right-hand side, towards the night table where I kept my gun.

I could hear another, softer noise. Breathing. He was a heavy breather. My room was pitch black; I could rely only on my sense of hearing. My left foot reached the edge of the mattress. That I might live an extra second or two.

I tensed, readying myself to roll from the bed.

Then came the explosion.

The gun went off and lit up the room like a flashcube. I couldn't be concerned whether I'd been hit. I rolled fast and hit the ground hard. My left hand clawed at the drawer, slithered inside, wrapped itself around the handle of my gun and thumbed off the safety. Twisting onto my back, I brought the gun to bear with three-point-nine pounds of pressure on a four-pound trigger just as the lights went on.

"I thought you white-eyes slept in jammies?"

It was Danny Many Guns. He had his left arm locked around the neck of Phillip P. Wilson, the sometimes inmate of Barbary Prison. A big, blue-black, nine mm Glock lay on my bed. Danny Many Guns held a flat knife blade against the base of Phillip P. Wilson's neck. Wilson outweighed Danny by a good fifty pounds but Danny had him up on tiptoe. Most people, when they put you in a neck lock, bring their arm around too far. The trick was to keep the bone in the forearm, in this case, Danny's right arm, straight across the front of the throat, against the windpipe. The right hand goes over the bend of the left arm, just above the elbow. You complete the lock by cupping the left hand around the back of their head. You don't squeeze. You simply press their head forward. The forearm completely blocks off the air supply. If you move your left hand behind your own head, as Danny did when he let the knife slip, it changes the grip to a hangman's noose. In less than a second, if Danny decided it was so, he could snap Wilson's neck and turn him into a paraplegic. Or worse.

I stood up slowly, my gun still firm on Wilson's heart.

"Jammies are for white-eyes with something to hide," I answered back.

"Clearly," Danny said, "you don't have much to worry about in that department."

"I was going to thank you for saving my life," I said, "but screw off. Weren't you a little late?"

I checked myself for a bullet hole.

"No." Danny shook his head. "His gun discharged after I had him." He pointed to the bullet hole in my ceiling. "See?"

After I got dressed and got rid of most of the beer, we sat Phillip P. Wilson in my bedroom chair and tried to interrogate him.

Tried because Phillip P. Wilson was not being cooperative.

I stopped counting after his tenth, "Fuck you!" and his ninth, "And your fucking horse!"

"He's not going to tell you anything," Danny ventured. "Let him go."

I wasn't sure I heard right but Danny stepped back to a less threatening stance. He leant against the wall and folded his arms.

"Let him go?" I said.

"Sure."

"Just let him leave?"

"Escort him to the front door and turn him loose."

I had no idea what Danny had in mind.

"And that would be a good idea because?" I asked.

"Because he was followed. Two cars parked both ends of the street. They tried not to let him know so they aren't backing him up. I think they are insurance."

"For whom?"

"Whoever sent him to kill you. They'll take care of him for messing up, then come back and take care of you."

I think Danny was right on the money. I moved the SIG Sauer from Wilson's heart to his head and nodded towards the bedroom door.

He shook his head.

"No, man. I'm not going out there."

"Yes, you are," I told him.

He turned to Danny.

"I ain't going out there. They'll kill me."

Danny shrugged like he'd lost interest. Wilson turned back to me.

"Listen. If I go out there and they see you're still alive, I'm dead meat."

"Tough."

"Jesus Christ!" He was angry but he was also scared.

"Who sent you?"

"If I tell you that, I'm signing my own death warrant."

"Either way, you're a dead man. On your feet."

He played for time.

"If I tell you, you've gotta help me get away. And my family."

"I can't promise anything."

"Then pull the fuckin' trigger 'cos it'll be a lot better way to die than what those bastards have planned."

"Who are they?"

"If I tell you, you promise you'll help me? Help my family get away?"

"I promise I'll listen. I promise I'll help if I can. That's as good a promise as you're going to get."

He thought about it for a full minute. Nobody spoke.

"Okay." He finally broke the silence. "Listen up good. They're prob'ly getting antsy out there. Come looking for me soon enough." He shook his head. "You don't know who you're messin' with. Neither of you."

We just stared at him, waiting for him to start talking.

And when he finally did, I wished I'd shot him instead.

Chapter Twenty-Four

"I HAVE A WIFE AND A KID. A daughter. She's fourteen. Help them if you won't help me. Okay?" He wrung his hands and I thought of Cindy and her daughter.

"Okay." I nodded my head and waited to hear what he had to say.

"The Barbary," he said, finally. "It's run by the warden, Jackson Varney. Jacko. And his son-in-law, Glen Pesta. They control everything that goes down in the joint. They can make your life sweet or they can make it a rotten, fuckin' hell." He paused a moment to reflect. "Jacko's a career criminal working for the justice department. He organizes the inmates into work gangs. Most of the cons are doing hard time. Five-year minimums. There's a lot of talent locked up in the Barbary. Jacko hand picks them to do jobs on the outside."

I couldn't quite believe what I was hearing yet it made perfect sense.

"He keeps the money and hands out favours. He only uses inmates with families on the outside. He has a gang of ex-cons working for him to keep everyone in line. He pays them to put pressure on your wife and kids. One time, a couple of guys grabbed their families instead of pulling a job, tried to make a run for it. They didn't get far. They took 'em to an empty warehouse. Kids and all. They locked them in and turned a pair of Rottweilers on them. They let the coyotes have what was left."

"I remember that," Danny said. "Three kids."

Wilson nodded.

"Jackson Varney did that?" I said.

"Yeah." He paused again. "He's an evil fuck. So's Glen Pesta. After I set up Joe Baker and Dick Wyman, I switched cars and took the money back to Varney. I got a three-day pass and a thousand bucks. Hardly seems worth it." He took a moment. "Your name came up after you visited Len at the tattoo place. That knife an' snake tattoo's a sort of badge of honour. Lot of ex-cons get it to show they done time in the Barbary. The ex-cons on Varney's payroll have two extra lines on the blade. Blood channels, they call 'em. So the blade comes out easier. They is all hard motherfuckers, those cons. They've all drawn blood, you know?"

I understood what he was talking about. The channel allows the blood to escape and stops the muscle from clamping up on the blade. Doug's tattoo had the extra lines. We were talking about some very nasty people here.

"Joe Baker had a tattoo," I said.

"Yeah. He was an inmate. I never knew him. He kept to himself. White guys don't play with brothers in the Barb. Anyway, he was out a month after I got jammed up. Dick Wyman was there before my time, so I never met him either."

"So who wants me dead?" I asked him.

"Jacko. Figures you got too close when you went to Len's place."

We were concerned about the time now. Two carloads of contract killers were parked on the street outside my house. We asked him about other robberies.

"That Brinks truck holdup two years ago? That was big. That was Jacko's deal. The casino heist last year? That was his, too. Jewellery heist back in February when they smashed their way through the store? That was one of his."

"Son of bitch." I shook my head. "You're talking millions," I said.

"Yeah. Millions."

"What happens when you don't show up?" Danny asked.

"They take my missus and my kid. They'll be watching them right now. They always watch your family when you're out."

"What will they do about me?"

"Send someone else," he said, like it was that obvious.

"Where does your family live?" I asked.

"Dover."

"Okay. Here's the plan," I said and Wilson sat in stony silence while I outlined my idea. It really wasn't much of an idea because it was full of ifs, ands and buts but it was the best idea I could think of in the time allowed.

I packed speed loaders for the SIG Sauer. Danny made a couple of phone calls to arrange transport while I poured a quart of old engine oil into an empty coffee can in the garage, in the dark, spilling more than the can would hold. I snapped the lid on real tight and wiped it clean. It stank.

"Are we ready?" I whispered, careful not to drip oil on my hardwood floor.

"Yes, Kemo Sabe," Danny said, playing Tonto to my Lone Ranger.

I once asked him what Kemo Sabe meant.

He told me.

"White Trash."

We left quietly, by the back door, under cover of darkness. Two streets over, a dark blue Ford Taurus was parked in the shadows, the keys under the driver's mat. When Danny opened the door, the interior light stayed off. Good planning. I began to feel better about the idea. We pulled away. Nobody followed us.

Getting better all the time.

Chapter Twenty-Five

PHILLIP P. WILSON'S WIFE'S NAME was Maria. His daughter was Melissa and they lived in a rented basement suite of a duplex in the Dover subdivision. It was all the rent they could afford.

"Do I get my gun back?" Wilson asked me as we drove.

"No."

By the time Danny dropped me at the lockup behind my office, a pale light washed over the eastern sky. I wheeled the Honda out and fired it up, jammed the helmet over my ears, gave Danny the thumbs up and tapped the shifter into first. She spat gravel from the back wheel as I tried to harness the one hundred and sixty horses. I kept my feet down until we hit the blacktop, then wound the throttle open and felt the front end going light as she tried to rotate around the back wheel. I had the coffee can full of oil balanced between my thighs.

Dover was maybe fifteen minutes away. We'd studied the map and we all knew where we were going and what we needed to do. We didn't dare risk phoning Wilson's wife in case they were tapping the line. The plan was to locate the ex-cons first. They shouldn't be hard to spot. There was no reason for them to be in hiding. Unless the ones who were watching Phillip P. Wilson realized he'd given them the slip and had alerted the ones watching his family.

I drove slowly down Phillip's wife's street. Outside her apartment, I passed a black Ford F150 truck with smoked rear windows. I angled my right-hand mirror up and out so I could see directly into the cab as I rode past them. I saw two heavy guys sitting in the front, smoking. One of them turned his head and it looked like he was speaking to someone in the back. I rode on, scanning the vehicles parked either side of the road. The rest of the vehicles were empty.

Danny was waiting on the next street over. I parked the bike, walked back to him and slid across the front seat.

"At least three people in a black F150 right outside his wife's place," I said and Phillip P. Wilson sucked air through clenched teeth. "I didn't see anyone else."

"We drove the back lane," Danny said. "There's a dark red Intrepid parked up behind the house. Two guys in the front seat."

"Get a number?"

He handed me a piece of paper with the licence number in his neat handwriting.

"We're running out of time," Wilson reminded us.

I phoned the cops. I gave them a fictitious name and an address on the next street over and told them about the dark red Intrepid parked in the back lane. I gave them the licence number and told them I'd seen the driver talking to a very young girl. Maybe eight or nine. And that I thought they had her in the car with them. I thought they were forcing her to do things she really didn't want to do.

I hung up.

We were ready to roll. Danny fired up the motor and I hurried back to the bike. I rode around the block, the coffee can balanced on the gas tank, and pulled over, a hundred yards behind the Ford truck. Danny passed me, approaching the F150. He drove past them slowly, as though looking for a parking spot. He stopped, put the car in reverse and tried to park in the impossibly tight space in front of the Ford. He backed in with a little too much power and smashed the left front fender of the F150. The driver's door opened and a big man stepped out. As he did so, Danny slammed the Taurus into drive and took off down the road. The big man stood for a moment before clambering back inside the truck. As the door swung shut, I pulled out a hundred yards back.

Danny made a screeching left turn at the end of the road and the F150 was in full flight, right behind him. I stayed fifty yards behind them both. They went four more blocks until they reached the four-way stop. Danny stopped the Taurus right on the stop line and waited. As the Ford pulled up behind him, I accelerated hard and closed the gap. The driver's door flew open a second time and so did the passenger side door but before they climbed out, Danny roared away again. The driver's door slammed shut just as I pulled alongside the truck and planted both feet either side of the bike. I ripped the plastic lid from the coffee can and dumped two quarts of thick black oil all over their windshield.

I barely had time to pull away when the driver shot forward, clipping my back wheel. The bike slid sideways under me but I knew enough to stay on the gas until the rear tire grabbed some traction, then snapped the throttle open, fishtailing hard down the road, the front wheel two feet off the ground. They chased me for a few hundred yards before the driver hit the wiper button.

The big blades smeared the thick, heavy oil in an impenetrable arc across the windshield. The driver nailed the brakes. He was blinded, almost a mile from Marie's home. Jazzed, I made a left, then another, arriving back at Marie's house ahead of Danny and Phillip. I jumped off the bike and ducked around back. A city cruiser with its party lights on was parked up behind the red Intrepid. Two men were spread-eagled on the hood.

Marie was surprised to see us, rubbing knuckles in her eyes, her hair a fright. There was no time for introductions, no time to pack. Melissa was still in bed. She looked stunned when Maria threw a coat over her shoulders and hauled her out of bed. Phillip threw her over his shoulder like a bag of groceries. We ran back down the walkway to the Taurus and hustled them into the back seat. Phillip jumped in and Danny pulled hard away from the house. I grabbed my helmet, straddled the Honda and rolled the power on.

The whole rescue had taken barely six minutes, beginning to end, and I was trembling from the rush of adrenaline.

Or maybe that was because now I had time to reflect on the consequences.

Chapter Twenty-Six

THE SECOND PART OF THE PLAN was to meet at Danny's apartment, assuming the first part had gone according to plan. I parked up facing the Bow River — a wide, almost flat-flowing shallow stream at this time of year. I kept a bike cover bungeed to the back seat and unhooked it, covering the bike and snapping the bungee cord across the back end to keep the cover in place. Satisfied the bike and my ZEN plate were covered, I took the stairs three at a time back up to Danny's apartment.

His condo overlooked the Bow River and the mountains to the west. It was clearly a million-dollar view, one that intimidated Maria and Melissa Wilson. Or maybe it was the height. Or perhaps it was Danny's taste in furnishing. There wasn't a single stick of furniture in Danny's apartment that had cost less than five figures. The big-screen TV was a flat-screen, plasma affair that took up most of one wall.

I studied Maria and Melissa Wilson. Maria wasn't as dark as her husband and Melissa was the colour of latte.

Her delicate features and thick dark eyelashes gave her a head start in the heartache stakes.

"Would you care for breakfast, Mrs. Wilson?" Danny the Butler said. She shook her head. "Melissa?" But she stayed close to her mother, clearly unnerved by Danny's grey eye. Or maybe it was the dark brown one. I asked him once if things looked any different out of one eye than the other.

"Yes," he told me. "Out of this one —" he pointed to the dark eye "— I see everything in black and white but out of this one —" he pointed to the other one "— I see everything in shades of grey."

He may have been pulling my leg.

"Now what?" Wilson asked.

"That depends," I answered. "Will Jackson Varney blow the whistle on your disappearance?"

"I doubt it. He'd have to say I escaped. That would show him in a bad light. There'd be an inquiry. He won't risk it. He'll put more pressure on the ex-cons to find me." He stared at me. "And you."

"I'm aware of that," I said.

Danny had been on the phone since we'd arrived. He hung up and turned to us. "Someone will be here in thirty minutes," he said. "They will drive you to a safe place. All three of you. You can stay together as a family. You'll be on a reserve, in a house by yourselves. Nobody will bother you. The kitchen will be stocked with food, the fridge too. When we resolve this problem, we'll see what can be done."

"Like what?" Wilson the Belligerent asked.

"We'll see," Danny the Inscrutable answered.

Few people knew of my connection to Danny Many

Guns. His apartment was registered to a numbered company and it's doubtful that Jackson Varney had the resources to track me to the condo. We were safe. For now. Danny made coffee and we stood looking out the window, not saying much. Phillip sat with his family on the chesterfield, talking quietly. When they left, Maria Wilson surprised us both and hugged us hard. "Thank you," she said and turned quickly away to hide the tears that welled in her eyes.

Phillip stood awkwardly, shifting from one foot to the other. Finally, he, too, stepped up to the plate and gave us both a handshake, which was preferable to a hug.

Then Danny returned his gun, a covert move I almost missed.

After he closed the door to his apartment, I stopped him.

"Was it loaded?" I asked.

"Such an untrusting soul," he said. "You want take-out for breakfast or do you trust my cooking?"

We ordered take-out. I was fresh out of trust that day.

Chapter Twenty-Seven

I TOOK OVER DANNY'S SPARE BEDROOM. Nosher and Splosher had agreed to do a drive-by for me. They reported back that my house and my office were staked out tighter than a duck's arse. I wondered if Jackson Varney was running short of ex-cons but he seemed to have an endless supply. I also wondered if I had bitten off more than I could chew.

Hot Wheels made the morning news. The local TV stations were milking the story. Amateur video film showed the police and firefighters opening up the hood with the Jaws of Life. The paramedics lifted Hot Wheels out. He was missing most of the fingers from his left hand and a few from his right. His left ear was missing along with a sizeable chunk of his hair. He looked like he'd been scalped. His lower lip looked strange, like it had been sliced off, and his teeth looked jagged beneath the blood. I don't think he had a chin anymore. His shirt was in tatters and there were angry burn marks over much of his body. Then the picture went fuzzy and you could hear the amateur videographer throwing up.

I phoned Cindy Palmer at home. It seemed like ages since I'd sat out on her deck and we'd had lunch. When she answered, I said "Hi," and right away she knew it was me.

"So," she said, "I hope you're phoning to invite me out for supper."

I said I'd love to but I had my hands full right now. We talked for a long time and she asked if I knew what had happened to Angie and the other girls. I told her I had a pretty good idea.

"Enough to disconnect the source?" she asked.

"More than enough," I told her.

I didn't elaborate. I just wanted to hear the sound of her voice, not darken her day with further atrocities. I promised I'd call her when things settled down and we'd definitely do dinner and a show. And anything else that she felt like doing.

When I hung up, I felt cheered — elated even. It had been a long dry spell. For both of us from the sound of it.

Later that morning, I phoned Dana Parker, she of the red hair and the smarty mouth.

"Any luck with those VIN numbers?" I asked.

"Don't you read your fax?"

Damn. The new fax machine was still in my Blazer. I asked her to re-fax it to Danny's place. She grumbled some more but she did it. A few minutes later, Danny's fax machine hummed and spat out several typed pages. I gathered them up and sat in Danny's huge leather chair to read them. They were a list of the names and addresses of the owners of all seven bikes, all Harleys. Only five of the seven had been reported stolen. I read through the list. Nothing jumped out at me, but when I saw the names of the owners who hadn't reported their bikes stolen, I got a thrill. The first name was Jimmie Faddon. Jimmie wasn't just a Harley owner; he was a Death's Head biker who got his name in the paper more often than the mayor. The other name was Bertrum Maurice Rarick, also known as Dirty Bertie. Well now, fancy that. Len and Doug had ripped off a pair of Harleys belonging to the Death's Head.

Opportunity knocks.

I left a note for Danny in case he came back before me and let myself out. Technically, I was still working for the Wymans but I had to protect myself too. Maybe I could give Len and Doug something more to worry about than messing with me. I uncovered the Blackbird, crammed the helmet down over my ears, snapped the dark visor shut and rolled on out of there. I knew the Death's Head had their clubhouse in Bowness, on the city's west side. It was a mix of older homes and miles of commercial and retail outlets. The clubhouse was an easy place to find. A bunch of hogs were parked on the road, on the sidewalk, in the front yard and maybe one or two up on the roof. For my trouble, I got the evil eye as I rode by slowly. I parked up around the corner and decided on a peace offering. I walked three blocks to the bakery and bought a dozen doughnuts, hot and sticky, fresh from the oven.

The guy who gave me the evil eye was sitting shotgun outside the house. It resembled an armoury more than a residence. There were no windows that I could see anywhere on the ground floor. The evil-eyed troll stuck his leg across the entrance, blocking my path.

"I bear gifts for the King," I announced.

"Fuck you. Fuck off."

"Where ignorance prevails, vulgarity invariably inserts itself," I said, though I doubt he was a Winston Churchill fan.

"I'll insert something, you don't get the fuck outa here," he said.

"I thought you guys liked doughnuts? Oh, wait. That's the other guys."

"I ain't telling you twice."

I tried a different tack.

"Is the man of the house in?" I said.

"Are you fuckin' deaf or just fuckin' stupid?" He stood up.

"I'm looking for Jimmie Faddon." I spoke over the top of the doughnut box. "I know who ripped off his Harley."

"I'll rip off your fuckin' head if you don't get outa here."

He made a threatening gesture but I could tell the smell of fresh doughnuts was breaking down his resolve.

"Let me guess," I said, opening the lid. "You're a jelly jam kinda guy."

He reached over the top of the doughnut box and grabbed my lapels. I mashed the box of warm doughnuts in his face. While he scraped doughnut crud from his eyes, I turned sideways and raked the outer edge of my boot hard down his shinbone and cracked the heel into his foot. He sucked in a big lungful of air. I hooked my right foot behind his knees and swept his feet out from under him. He landed heavily on his back and I heard his lungs collapse with an explosive whoosh. He tried to grab my foot and I kicked him hard in the ribs.

"Where's this hospitality you guys are famous for?"

I stepped over him and pushed the front door open with my toe.

"Yoo-hoo!" I called out into the darkness.

When nobody answered, I moved farther into the room. I counted at least five Harleys parked up inside. Ahead of me ran a steep wooden staircase without carpet or handrail. Another violation of the building code. I plunged ahead. In for a penny, in for a pound.

I hadn't expected this many people to be up and around so early. There must have been a dozen bikers sitting around what normal folks might call the living room. It looked like a council of war.

At least half of them stood up and crowded me. I had spotted Jimmie Faddon from across the room. I spoke directly to him over a dozen bearded and hostile faces.

"I know who stole your hog," I said. "And Bertie's."

At first, I thought they weren't going to stop. I thought they were simply going to beat me to a pulp and stomp my bones through the floorboards. And maybe they were but Jimmie's voice carried authority.

"Stop!"

They stopped. But if looks could kill, I was already a dead man. Jimmie stepped forward, pushing a pair of them out of his way to get to me. We were about the same size but Jimmie Faddon had at least three centuries of living on me.

"Who?"

"Len and Doug," I said. "Len runs a tattoo parlour in Vic Park."

"I know 'em," someone said but Jimmie ignored him.

"Says who?"

I pulled the two VIN tags from my pocket.

"I broke into their place a few days ago. I was looking for something. I found a tin of these."

Jimmie never looked down.

"Who says I had a bike stolen?"

"I have a friend in admin. She ran the numbers. These were registered to you and Bertie Rarick. You never reported them stolen. This is just between us girls."

He thought about that for a moment.

"What do you want?"

"Future considerations," I said, hedging my bets.

Just then, with heavy footsteps and much swearing, the shotgun kid from outside blundered into the room. He came straight at me, swinging wildly.

His left fist glanced off my right shoulder. His right fist stung me a good shot high on the cheekbone. Duck and weave. I slipped his next right and tucked my elbows in, then, when he stepped inside, I clenched my fists and drove a sharp right into his solar plexus. He was in better shape than I realized. The blow hurt him but didn't wind him as it should. He moved in again and I hit him three fast blows to the body, backed him up and snapped off a quick shot to the head, lining him up for a left hook. He stepped back quickly, moving out of range, then rushed me again but this time Jimmie Faddon stepped in. He hit the man a brutal, blind-side right hook that levelled him to the floor.

"Your job's to keep people out," he said but the man was past caring. He lay on the floor, ignored by all. Jimmie turned to me. "Are you really this stupid?"

"I'm just pure of heart," I said. "If someone ripped off my bike, I'd want to know who did it." I handed him the tags. "It's the least I can do."

Jimmie considered this.

"Come up here again, we'll stomp your ass."

"Yeah, well, I'd have called first but you guys aren't exactly in the Yellow Pages."

"Wait outside 'til someone invites you up."

"Understood." I nodded.

"How'd you get past Spider?" He nodded at the man on the floor.

I looked down at the man.

"He has a weakness," I said.

"Yeah?"

"Doughnuts."

Chapter Twenty-Eight

I STAYED AT DANNY'S APARTMENT for the next three days. Nosher and Splosher took turns cruising the neighbourhood and there was no loss of interest in finding me.

"Different crew this morning," Nosher reported. "This Jacko's got a regular army."

That's what I was afraid of. Apart from a change of clothes, there was nothing in my house that I needed right now. My office had been refurbished, without furniture. Nothing I needed from there. My phone was call-forwarded to my cell. I returned calls, did the *Calgary Herald* crossword puzzle, in ink, and watched daytime TV. I was getting cabin fever. I'd have been better off locked up in the Barbary.

We could, of course, go to the police. But without hard evidence, there was virtually nothing they could do. We could have gone to the media but what good would that do? By now, the bad guys knew that I knew who they were. The media weren't going to protect me when it hit the fan.

I was getting restless. I preferred taking my fight to the enemy. Of course, that was a good way to get myself killed. I had deliberately resisted contacting either Joe Baker or Dick Wyman for the last five days because Jackson Varney was, undoubtedly, having them watched as well.

Danny brought some good news. Velvet was getting better. She'd agreed to go back home to Vancouver. Try again to be a daughter. The sweat lodge healing had worked its magic. Pity we couldn't have taken Angie there. She was being moved to a full-care facility later in the week. I'd check on her in a few more days.

Early the next morning, I picked up the *Calgary Herald* and carried it through to the breakfast nook. I was flipping through it, looking for the crossword puzzle on the comics page, and came across a headline in the City section that caught my attention.

TWO MEN BEATEN AND MULTILATED

Two men were found badly beaten late last night at a house they rent in Victoria Park. A police spokesman revealed that both men had had their hands chopped off. The victims have been identified as Leonard Mitchell and Douglas Malcolm McDonald, both of Calgary. Both men are known to the police and the assault is believed to be gang-related. Anyone with information about this crime is urged to contact the police, or to call Crime Stoppers. All calls are treated confidential.

I read it again. Someone chopped off their hands. I was having trouble getting my head around that. This is Canada, after all. We don't go around lopping off body parts. I tried to imagine how it went down. What had I expected? I guess a good old-fashioned ass whooping or maybe, just maybe, a bullet to the head, which would have been deserved. But to chop off their hands. I felt momentarily guilty. Then I thought about Angie and all the other girls they had turned into vegetable delight. After that, I thought they were lucky to have their hands chopped off. If I'd been there, I'd have lopped off their heads.

Something here had tweaked my curiosity. My problem was not being mobile. Since I had such a memorable bike, to say nothing of the vanity plate, I couldn't risk using it again. My Blazer sat outside my house, guarded by half a dozen ex-cons. Renting a car seemed like a bad idea since credit card transactions were traceable, especially by the bad guys. Danny had suggested borrowing a car but I'd be front and centre behind the windshield and hard to miss. Besides, I had involved enough people in this already.

I had an idea how I could be mobile, but it was a little risky. Okay, it was more than a little risky but there was a certain poetry about it that appealed to me.

And you know how I love poets.

Chapter Twenty-Nine

TRICKED OUT IN RUNNERS, shorts, a red sweatshirt, a white baseball hat, sunglasses, a fanny pack and a four-day stubble, carrying a plastic bottle of water, I looked like any other jogger. I'd raided Danny's fridge for high-energy snacks, since I'd skipped lunch, and took something that might have been beef jerky, a handful of nuts and raisins, an apple and some tea biscuits. Danny had an odd taste in food. I ran from downtown to Len and Doug's place. Soaked in sweat, I was just another invisible jogger in a city of thousands.

The yellow DO NOT CROSS crime scene tape was visible from the corner. Staying on the sidewalk, I jogged towards their place. There were no police cars, marked or unmarked, anywhere on the street. As I drew level with the house, I glanced under the front stoop. The dog had gone. I stopped and leaned forward, hands on my thighs as if I was winded from the run, and when I straightened up, I was on the other side the yellow tape. I moved quickly down the side of the house and ducked around back. There was no tape across the back where I pushed my way upside the garage and stood by the closed window. To my left I saw the electrical box, beneath it, the meter. I pulled my knife from the fanny pack and was about to work the latch again when I noticed that the meter was turning. Someone was inside using the power. I froze, watching the disc revolve in the meter. It was painfully slow. I tried to imagine what would draw such a small amount of electricity. A light? I risked a look but couldn't see any lights on from where I was standing.

Think, dammit.

While I stood there, knee deep in weeds, attracting flies, the power went off, the wheel stopped turning.

I visualized each room and when I visualized the kitchen, I realized what it was.

Just the fridge.

I stuck the knife into the window space and worked the latch free. It made a sound like a locomotive. Don't people maintain their homes anymore? I pushed the curtain aside and listened closely. Nothing. I stepped over the sill but left the curtain open to eke out what little light I could. I was looking, of course, for transportation. Len or Doug's Harley would do nicely. After all, they wouldn't be using them, would they?

Unfortunately, someone must have had the same idea. There were no assembled, ready-to-run Harleys anywhere in the garage. Given a week or two, I could probably assemble a custom bike from all the parts but I didn't have that much time.

As I stood in the darkened garage, I became aware of a smell that hadn't been there on my last visit. I knew what it was. It was the smell of human blood. I looked around the floor. There were dark blotches. Lots of them. Not pools of blood but dried, crusted blood that looked like someone had tried to clean up. I wondered if this was where they had chopped their hands off. Had the cops found their hands? I hoped so.

I thought there was something, however, that the police might have overlooked.

Len's address book.

It was exactly where I'd left it. Hidden under the corner of the chesterfield, surrounded by a litter of beer cans and an overflowing ashtray. I reached for it gingerly, half-expecting it to come out with a severed hand attached. When I first read it, I'd been curious about the letter B after Joe Baker's name. I sat down on the chesterfield and flipped open the book. I turned to the *R*s but there was nothing under Richard Wyman. But under the *D*s there was Dick W with a letter B. I thumbed through the rest of the book. There were maybe four dozen names with the letter B after them and maybe half of them were circled. So, it was some sort of code. A plain B or a circled B.

To be, or not to be?

Was B for Barbary?

I was just starting to feel smug when I heard a noise that shouldn't have been there. A rattle. A metal-on-metal sound that raised the hairs on the back of my neck. I shoved the address book into the fanny pack and looked up as the curtain moved.

It was the dog.

He had smelled me. And he had been living in a house with pools of human blood. He bared his teeth and his hackles came up as he pushed farther into the room. A cross between a German shepherd and something really mean and nasty. There was blood on his fur. From lapping up the blood to slake his hunger. He dropped low, getting ready to attack. I tucked my legs under me like a fourteen-year-old girl reading a library book.

"Good doggie." I spoke quietly but to no avail.

Long ropes of spittle hung from his jaw. His eyes gleamed red in the dim light, his teeth a filthy yellow. He was getting ready to spring. My knife was in the fanny pack. I risked a tiny movement towards it. He growled a warning, deep in his rib cage.

"Good boy."

I hardly dared to breathe.

My fingers reached inside the fanny pack. The knife was at the bottom. The dog moved closer, never taking his eyes off my throat. He looked very hungry.

My fingers brushed something.

Danny's beef jerky.

I pulled a piece out. The dog stopped. His eyes flicked to my fingers.

"Here," I said and gingerly tossed the first piece towards him.

He watched it fall to the carpet. His teeth were more pronounced. Edging forward, full of canine suspicion, he risked a sniff. His tongue came out. He sniffed it again. Then licked it.

It disappeared down his throat.

"Good boy."

I threw him a larger piece. And another. The fourth piece he caught in midair.

"Good dog," I encouraged him.

His hackles went down a millimetre. I was about half-way through the jerky. I held the next piece in my fingers. He inched forward, snatched it right out of my hand.

"Good dog!"

He took the next two pieces. I curled the last piece inside my fist. He came closer. It occurred to me this was a good way to lose an arm. He tried to shove his snout into my closed fist. While he did so, I risked moving my thumb. I traced the length of his jaw.

"Good dog," I encouraged him some more.

Slowly, I let him nuzzle my hand and he let me stroke his fur. He slurped the last of the jerky and didn't move when I continued to stroke him. The hackles were almost down. I risked moving a leg, the right one, because it had fallen asleep. He allowed me that much. I turned the dog tags around. In order to read his name, I had to put my face very close to his. He bristled.

Me too.

"That's okay, Duke." I soothed him some more.

He licked the beef jerky residue from my palm and I petted him some more. After another few minutes, he let me put my other leg to the floor in exchange for the tea biscuits.

"Still hungry, Duke?" He cocked an ear. "Dinner?" He cocked the other one. "Come on, then."

He let me stand and I walked slowly and very carefully to the kitchen. There was nothing edible in the fridge. They must shop at the same store as Danny. In a cupboard over the sink I found a row of dog food in yellow and orange cans.

Duke knew he'd hit the mother lode because he backed up, barking, and his tail went crazy. Eight cans of dog meat and not a can opener anywhere.

He followed me into the garage. I used a cold chisel and hammer and the moment I punched the first hole in the lid, he wouldn't leave me alone. It took me about ten minutes to open all eight cans and Duke about thirty seconds to eat them. I found his empty water bowl and fixed him a long, cold drink of water. He let me wash the blood from his fur. I found a towel and rubbed him dry. The poor thing was starved of food and affection. He lay on his back, writhing back and forth while I rubbed his chest and his belly.

When I went back into the living room to retrieve the fanny pack, he followed me like I was his new best friend.

Clearly, I couldn't leave him there. I fashioned a leash from a length of rope and took him out the same way I'd come in. He wasn't the best-behaved dog and he kept tugging on the leash but when I picked up the pace to a fast jog, he stayed alongside me without tripping me over. On the way back to Danny's place, I thought about my next move.

It was even riskier than this one.

Chapter Thirty

DUKE LAY ON DANNY'S FRONT DOORMAT while I changed my clothes. Jeans, a black T-shirt, black baseball hat, my Alpinestar boots and dark sunglasses. I walked him back downstairs and over to the taxi stand on Fourth Avenue. The first three cabbies refused to take both of us but the fourth agreed to do it, at double the fare. I told him Duke was my seeing-eye dog.

When we reached the address in Bowness, the driver looked decidedly uneasy.

"Keep the meter running," I told him and stepped out, tugging Duke from the back of the cab.

Spider wasn't on duty, which was probably a blessing. For both of us. There were two Death's Heads on guard duty. They glared at me as I approached.

"I need to talk to Jimmie," I told them.

I moved my glasses off my face so they could see me more clearly but they already knew who I was. Duke sat obediently on my foot. One of the bikers leaned in the open door and yelled.

"Yo, Bertie!"

The biggest, meanest-looking badass biker I'd ever seen stuck his head around the clubhouse door. It was a head that was completely shaved. His ears were covered in studs and rings and enough other stuff to cause a meltdown in a metal detector. He wore a filthy pair of denim jeans and a filthy, wife-beater T-shirt. I couldn't begin to imagine where he shopped to find something that would wrap around his enormous gut.

"The fuck y'want?" he growled at Biker Two.

Biker Two stabbed his bearded chin towards me. "This guy's looking for Jimmie. He's the one found who stole yer bike."

Bertie looked at me. "So?"

"I'm here to see Jimmie," I said.

"Jimmie don't wanna see you." He reached out and poked me with a finger the size of a beef sausage. "Fuck off."

"He owes me a favour."

"Jimmie don't owe any favours. Now get the fuck outta here 'fore I crush your fuckin' skull."

This wasn't quite going according to plan.

"Give Jimmie a message for me," I said and the Jolly Green Giant reached out and laid his hand atop my head like it was a basketball.

"You don't get any more chances," he said and I felt his fingers tighten on my skull.

I hoped Duke would spring into action but he seemed oblivious to the plight of his new best friend. As Bertie tightened his grip, I felt the plates of my skull rub together. Not long now, I thought, and I'll just pass out and die. I heard the deafening roar of a Harley chopper pulling onto the lot. Or maybe it was all the blood leaving my brain. They sound a lot alike. I tried to turn my head to see who it was but the best I could manage was a half-hearted eye swivel.

"Yo, Bertie. Watcha got there?"

It was Jimmie.

Thank God.

Or maybe not.

"A pimple," Bertie said. "Stay back, I'm gonna pop it."

He wasn't kidding. I squeezed my eyes shut against the pain and when I opened them again, Jimmie Faddon was leaning into my face.

"You again," he said.

"Yeah," I think I said but it sounded like a whale fart.

"You bring doughnuts?"

I tried to shake my head, but it was like it was clamped in a vise.

"What'cha want?"

"Future consideration," I said but nobody understood me.

"What?"

I reached up and wrapped my puny fingers around Bertie's rolling-pin sized pinkie.

"Future consideration." I tried again and bent Bertie's finger sideways against the joint.

It wouldn't budge.

"Future what?" Jimmie said.

"Con-sid-er-ation."

I gave another reef on Bertie's fat finger and this time it

moved a quarter inch.

"Hey." Bertie slapped me across the back of the head with his free hand. "Quit that!"

"I need that favour," I told Jimmie, sounding like I'd been inhaling helium.

"Stand back," Bertie said. "I'm gonna pop him good."

I think I started screaming first and then Bertie joined in and it was hard to tell us apart. He let go of my head so suddenly, I almost fell over. I turned back to see what all the fuss was about. Duke had his teeth in Bertie's prodigious ass.

"Get that fuckin' dog offa me!"

Bertie was moving in a great, wide circle. Duke was tugged around sideways but that just made it more of a game. His back legs left the ground but he wasn't letting up anytime soon.

More bikers spilled out, enjoying Bertie's plight.

"What'cha want?" Jimmie Faddon asked me, yelling above the noise.

"A bike!" I told him. "And I need to look the part!"

"Why?"

I shook my head. "None of your business!" I said.

Jimmie glanced over at Bertie and the dog.

"Call him off!"

"I'll call mine off if you'll call yours off!"

"Yeah." Jimmie nodded.

Easier said than done. I tried to grab Duke as he swung by sideways but I missed him. I waited until he came around again and he whacked me across the legs and almost knocked me down. As he came back around, I grabbed Bertie by the shoulders. It was like grabbing the side of a cow.

"Stand still!" I yelled at him.

He slowed, more from fatigue than anything I said. I managed to grab Duke.

"Let go!"

Duke shook his head and that made Bertie even madder.

"Drop it!" I yelled and Duke let go.

He backed up and stood his ground, snarling when Bertie tried to kick him in the head.

"I wouldn't do that," I said. "He's a testicle-trained attack dog."

Bertie's face was flame red. He brought his hands out front and there was blood on them.

"Fuckin' dog! Ripped a piece outta my ass!" He glared at me. "You ain't leavin' here alive!"

Jimmie shook his head. It was something to see. Little Jimmie holding off four hundred pounds of animal fat and testosterone with a shake of his head.

"Do I still need the taxi or not?" I asked Jimmie.

Jimmie looked over at the cabbie and waved him away. He left without being paid.

"Your dog?"

"Technically, he's yours."

"How's that?"

"He was Len's."

"Must'a bit the hand that fed him." He didn't even crack a smile. "What do I wanna dog for?" he asked.

"He's a good guard dog."

"So's Bertie."

"Cost less to feed Duke, though."

Jimmie dropped his hand by his side. Duke sniffed it cautiously. Jimmie roughed his mane and Duke leaned into his leg.

"He likes you."

"That's 'cos I'm loveable."

"Do we have a deal?"

"You wanna bike?"

"Yes. Len's will do. Or Doug's."

"And rags?"

"Need to look the part."

"Okay." Jimmie Faddon nodded. "The bike's yours." He looked over at Dirty Bertie. "Get him what he needs." He turned back to me. "One thing. You wanna be an honorary member, you gotta join the club."

I figured that was coming.

"Deal?" he asked.

"Deal," I said.

We clacked knuckles like prehistoric cavemen signing a contract. He looked down at Duke.

"You're a real ball buster, eh Duke?"

Duke licked Jimmie's fingers. Friends for life. The rotten turncoat.

"Come on."

I followed him inside and he called the other bikers to order. The deal was simple. If I was riding a hog and looking like a Death's Head, I had to be initiated.

"Jeans off."

I took them off and Jimmie tossed them on the floor. A dozen bikers stood around them in a loose semi-circle. Then they all unzipped and peed on my jeans. It was a Death's

Head rite of passage. A real Death's Head biker would wear them forever and never wash them but they only required me to wear them, wet and warm and stinky as hell, to ride away from the clubhouse.

When I left Bowness twenty minutes later, my own mother wouldn't recognize me. The Death's Head had thrown in a sleeveless denim jacket, a ragged and smelly T-shirt, a do-rag and a helmet that had seen better days during World War One. The DOT sticker on the back was a joke. I wore a studded leather wrist wrap and a spiked leather choker. I refused to give up the Alpinestars though. I wasn't allowed to wear anything that said Death's Head but I looked the part without infringing their copyright. You don't think they own the name? Think again.

Jimmie stood before me as I mounted Len's Harley.

"When this is over, you come back and tell me about it. Deal?"

"Deal."

We didn't clack knuckles this time. As an honorary member, my word was now my bond.

As I chugged away from the clubhouse, I saw Duke cock his leg on Jimmie's Harley.

Jimmie would probably promote him.

Chapter Thirty-One

YOU CANNOT IMAGINE HOW IT FEELS wearing tight-fitting jeans soaked in other men's piss. My genitals had performed an incredible shrink in their attempt to stay dry. To no avail. The warm wind helped dry the worst of it but my ass was still soaked and I smelled worse than anything I could imagine. I looked the part, though. Riding the Honda, I was used to a certain reaction from other road users. On the Harley, evil personified, I gained a whole different respect. Motorists refused to make eye contact. Woman drivers, especially with young children in the car, gave me a wide berth. Regular bikers, who would normally give me the left-handed side salute, never bothered, knowing I wouldn't return the gesture. So I waved the friendly gesture for the hell of it and most of them looked surprised enough to fall off their bikes.

I rode around until my jeans were mostly dry, then headed over to Joe Baker's house. He'd given me his address before we left Tony Roma's patio three lifetimes ago. I cruised slowly down his block.

There were two of them parked across the street from

Joe Baker's house. They watched me park up but didn't get too excited. There was a soft-tail Harley parked in Joe's drive. I rang the doorbell and when Joe Baker answered, I stepped inside and pushed the door shut before he could stop me.

"Relax, Joe," I told him and took off the helmet. Even then, it took him a moment.

"Je-sus H. Christ," he said. "What the hell are you doing? And what's that fuckin' stench?"

"I'm incognito," I said. "Figured your house was being watched."

"Them assholes," he said. "Day and night."

"They're ex-cons, right?"

He looked at me.

"Right."

"I figure your phone's tapped, too," I told him.

"No surprise there."

"If we ride, will they follow us?"

"Haven't so far but I've only been out on my own."

"Let's do this, then. I'll leave, you follow in about fifteen minutes."

"Make your point," Joe said.

"I got a lot to tell you."

He looked me up and down.

"I'll bet you do."

We planned to meet about a mile from his house. I felt their eyes on me as I walked back to the bike. I kicked it over three times. It wouldn't start. Damned Harleys. I'd probably flooded it. I kicked it over some more with the throttle shut until it finally spluttered to life. I was breathing hard as

I toed it into first and moved away from the curb. I couldn't tell if they were following me or not because the damned mirrors vibrated so badly, everything behind me was a blur. I hit the stop sign and had a quick look back. Nobody. I pulled across the junction and rode up a long, winding hill and parked up where Joe was supposed to meet me. He took longer than fifteen minutes and I was getting worried until I saw him chugging up the hill.

"Couldn't start the bike," he said.

I watched the road behind him. Nobody had followed him either. We rode for a few miles, pulling off along a deserted strip of highway on the outskirts of the city. I told Joe Baker most of what had happened in the last few days. He let me talk, hardly interrupting except to clarify a point. When I finished, he sat astride his bike and gazed off into the distance.

"So." he finally spoke. "How you gonna get my money back?"

Chapter Thirty-Two

I WAS BACK AT DANNY'S APARTMENT. The trip in the elevator had been interesting. The couple waiting to go up declined the opportunity to ride with me. The lady riding up from the underground parking lot almost twisted her ankle vacating the elevator the moment I stepped in and the man who boarded on the third level looked as though he was going to have a heart attack before he reached his floor.

Danny was home, which made for some interesting dialogue. I stripped off the jeans, T-shirt and underwear, double bagged them and dropped them down the garbage chute. I showered long enough to drain the hot water system for the entire building. I scrubbed every part of my body until it was pink and some parts I scrubbed until they were red. After about an hour, I began to feel a little less dirty. I towelled off gently and dressed in fresh, clean clothes. It was an absolute joy to wear clean underwear. There was a note on the fridge. "Back tomorrow." I hoped he'd left me sufficient food in the fridge to last until then.

I sat on Danny's chesterfield and waited for my phone

to ring. Joe Baker had agreed to contact Dick Wyman and bring him up to speed on the situation. I was expecting him to call my cell anytime.

The thing that bothered me the most was the army of ex-cons that Jackson Varney had at his disposal. They were everywhere. I dug through the fanny pack I'd been wearing when I met Duke and pulled out Len's address book. I went through it, page by page, taking a note of the names that had the letter B ascribed to them. There were forty names in all, fifteen with just a regular B and twenty-five with the B circled. From the sheer number, I guessed the circled ones were Varney's ex-cons for hire.

While Phillip P. Wilson was with us, he gave us a good description of Varney and his son-in-law. I was planning my next move when my cell phone rang.

It was Joe.

"I talked with Dick Wyman," he said. "He's in."

"He's in what?"

"In with whatever you're planning to do next," Joe said.

"Good," I answered.

"So," Joe said. "What *are* you planning to do next?"

"Storm the prison."

"Yeah. That sounds like a plan you might come up with, you fuckin' dickweed."

"You've got a better one?"

"No."

"Me neither."

"When you do, call me."

He hung up.

And I thought storming the prison was a good plan.

Chapter Thirty-Three

IT WAS LATE. Or maybe it was early. The bedside clock said three thirty-five a.m. My cell phone was ringing. I struggled to find it on the night table in Danny's spare bedroom. I'd spent most of the night thinking about what I really should do next. As far as the Wymans were concerned, I felt I'd fulfilled my obligation to them. I'd traced the money. Getting it back wasn't part of the deal. My main concern now was staying away from Jacko and his ex-cons. They could wait me out forever. I needed to turn over what I had to the authorities. Which wasn't very much. And would take a few years to investigate. Meanwhile, I'd still be a marked man.

Damned if you do, damned if you don't.

I found the cell phone.

"Yeah?"

My voice was thick from sleep, my head fuzzy.

"Dancer?"

"Yeah. Who's this?"

"Mine to know, yours to find out."

I glanced down at the call display but it just said Private

Name, Private Number.

"It's three-thirty in the morning," I said. "Playtime's over."

"For you it is."

"Who is this?"

"We've got your girlfriend."

It stopped me cold.

"I don't have a girlfriend," I said, carefully.

"And her kid."

Cindy.

I went numb.

"Who the hell is this?"

Click.

I was wide awake now. I dialled Cindy's home number by heart. It rang four times before the answer machine kicked in.

"Cindy! If you're there, pick up. It's Eddie. Pick up, Cindy!"

I phoned four times but nobody picked up. I phoned the Rockyview Emergency Admitting number. Someone named Vicky answered.

"Is Cindy Palmer working tonight?"

"Cindy? I don't think so. Can you hold a moment?"

"Yes."

She kept me on hold for almost three minutes. A lifetime. My heart was banging out of my chest.

"Hello?"

"Yes?"

"She's not working."

"I need to reach her. It's a family emergency."

"Oh. Well, she called in earlier. She's taking a few days off. Maybe a week. She said she was visiting family in B.C."

"Do you have a number where she can be reached?"

"Hold on."

Only two minutes this time.

"We only have her home number and we're not allowed to give it out."

"I have it. Does she have a cell?'

"If she does, we don't have that number."

I hung up. It took me one minute to dress. I grabbed the Honda key, to hell with whoever might be looking for me. I ripped the cover off the bike, threw it in an untidy heap and hit the starter. Hondas like a moment to warm up. The hell with that. I almost dropped it as I turned from the parking lot onto the road. I ignored almost everything, speed limits, stop signs, red lights and other road users. I doubt the front wheel touched the pavement. When I reached Cindy's condo, I parked as close as I could. I rang the bell and pounded on the door. A light went on at the neighbour's but Cindy's house remained in darkness. I pounded on the door again, risking the neighbour's wrath, then ran round the block and came around the back. I hopped the back gate and cupped my hands over the kitchen window. The place was in darkness. I could hear a noise. A steady hum. It was the heater for the hot tub. B.C. be damned. Who goes away and leaves the hot tub heater running?

There was a quiet squeak from somewhere below me and Norman stepped through the pet door. She blinked in the moonlight, then came over and rubbed herself against me. I bent down and rubbed her ears.

If only she could speak.

By the time I left, the neighbour had called the police. I kept the speed down as I passed them and they ignored me. They knew they had no chance of catching me anyway. I took a detour on the way back to Danny's and what I saw confirmed what I already knew.

I was back at Danny's by five o'clock. Before I left, I had Star 69ed the incoming call but of course, it refused to give up the identity of the early morning caller.

Now, of course, I knew who had her for sure. Cindy and her daughter. What was her name?

Lindsay.

I phoned the Barbary.

Yeah.

Let's storm the prison.

Because now it's personal.

Chapter Thirty-Four

"BARBARY FEDERAL," a man with a deep voice answered the phone.

I was surprised there was anyone manning the switchboard at five in the morning.

"Let me speak with Warden Varney."

"The warden isn't here right now, sir."

I racked my brains for his brother-in-law's name.

"Is Pesta there? Glen Pesta?"

"Sorry, no. Can you try back in a few hours? Maybe after nine?"

"Do you have a home number for either of them?"

"Who's calling?"

I hung up.

I realized how they had traced Cindy. I had made an hour-long call to her on my cell phone. They must have access to my cell phone records and traced her number. Maybe they had someone on the inside or maybe they applied a little external pressure or maybe they hacked into the phone company's computers. However they had done it, they had tracked down

162

Cindy Palmer through my stupidity. I hadn't considered calling her on my cell a risk to either one of us. Clearly, Varney's contacts went much further and far deeper than I imagined. Now they had her. What did they want in return?

I could guess.

Me.

So let the games begin.

My next call was to Danny's cell phone. I left a message for him to call me. It took less than a minute and he sounded awake and alert.

"You're sure that's who it is?" he said.

"Varney? Who else could it be?"

"You've made some strange enemies over the years. Lots of them."

No argument there. But this was different. The timing was too coincidental to be anyone but Varney.

"Besides," I told him, "I made a detour on the way back from Cindy's house."

"To where?'

"My place. Nobody's watching it anymore. He's pulled them off. He doesn't need them now that he has Cindy. And her daughter."

"Where are they?'

"I don't know. Could he keep them at the prison? It's a man's prison. I hate to think he'd keep them there." I was having a hard time keeping my emotions in check.

"I doubt he would," Danny said. "They could identify him from their surroundings."

Right. Unless he was planning not to let them leave — alive.

"Stay put," Danny said. "I'm on my way."

He hung up and left me with my thoughts, which were getting nastier by the minute. I wished I could reach out and assure Cindy and her daughter that I would not rest until they were both safe again.

I thought about calling Cindy's ex-husband, Lindsay's father. The cop. But Palmer was her maiden name. I could have tracked him down, though.

Maybe I should have.

Chapter Thirty-Five

WHILE I WAITED for Danny, I scoured the phone book, looking for a listing under Jackson Varney or Glen Pesta. I searched the Calgary listings first, then every small town within a fifty-mile radius. I found nothing. It made sense that men in their position would keep their home phone number private.

I called Danny back. Since we did not know where Varney or Pesta lived, we would need to watch the prison and follow them home from work. It was our only hope.

Danny arrived in time to save me from driving my head through the wall. He moved some expensive art from the coffee table and unrolled a map of Rocky View, where the Barbary was located. Land in Western Canada is divided into vertical columns, called ranges, and horizontal columns, called townships. Each column is six miles across. Where they intersect, they form a six by six mile grid. Thirty-six square miles. Each square mile is a section of land and each section is numbered one through thirty-six. Each section, is divided into four quarters, the northeast, northwest, southeast and southwest quarters. If you have the range and township numbers, the section number and the quarter location, you can locate any property to within a quarter mile. Most of the roads run straight, either vertically or horizontally, to form a huge grid.

The Barbary Prison occupied a complete section, one mile by one mile, six hundred and forty acres. There was only one road in and out of the prison. The road came in from the east, ran parallel to the southern edge for almost a mile, then swung due north up to the prison gates. That was as far as it went. According to the map, the land to the north, east and south was farmland, not yet subdivided into dozens of yuppie acreages. This would make approaching the prison very difficult, if not impossible. The sections of land immediately west of the prison were a different colour on the map than most of the other sections. They were darker.

"What does that mean?" I pointed to the group of darker coloured squares.

"Leased land," Danny said. "Theoretically, it's public land."

"Theoretically?"

"Yes. You can cross it without trespassing."

"But?"

Sometimes it was like pulling teeth.

"It's ranching country. Ranchers lease this land to graze their cattle."

"So?"

"It's also bear country. And moose habitat."

"Moose habitat?" He made it sound like an upscale Ikea store.

"And elk. And bulls."

"Wild animals?"

"Inside and out," he said.

"And if we come across any wild animals?"

"Shoot them."

I wasn't sure if he was being funny. Or which wild animals he was talking about.

We studied the map a little longer but it had revealed all there was to see. We needed a topographical map to understand the lie of the land but it would be easier to drive west of the prison and approach it on foot.

With a big wild-animal gun.

Chapter Thirty-Six

It was noon by the time we were organized and ready to roll. Phillip P. Wilson had given us a detailed description of Warden Varney and his son-in-law, Glen Pesta. We recruited Joe Baker and Dick Wyman to help with the stakeout. Since they had both spent time in the Barbary, they both knew Jacko and his son-in-law by sight. Danny drove his yellow Hummer and we picked up Dick and Joe along the way.

"A bit fuckin' conspicuous, ain't we?" Joe said as he climbed in.

"We won't be driving anywhere near the prison," Danny replied.

"So how we gettin' there?"

"How d'ya think?" Danny fired back and Joe made a face.

"Aw, fuck."

Clearly, Joe wasn't a hiker.

We drove west on Highway 1 for twenty minutes until Danny made a right turn and cut through reservation land — Indian territory. The land had begun turning brown under the heat of the long summer sun. A rooster tail of grey dust followed us along the gravel roads. We crested a series of hills, each one taking us a little higher, until we reached the turnoff that Danny had marked on the map. He swung the Hummer off the road and we bounced gently across a field of native grass, rolling downhill towards a forest of dark pines. We drove along the edge of the forest, bearing left all the way until we were out of sight of the gravel road high above us. Danny turned the Hummer into the trees and the interior grew dark and the mood turned sombre. We drove a hundred yards into the forest until the trees conspired against us. But no matter. We were invisible to anyone outside the forest — and anyone in it.

We stood around the hood as Danny unfolded the map.

"We're here." He stabbed a finger at the map. "The Barbary's there." He stabbed at a square, miles to the east of where we stood.

"Aw, shit," Joe complained. "It's fuckin' miles."

"We'll rendezvous here." Danny pointed to a spot half a mile from the Barbary fence line. "No need to risk being seen."

"Is it all forest?" Dick Wyman asked. It was a reasonable question.

"Partly," Danny said, nodding. "The first two miles are forest, then we're on government leased land. We have two miles of native grassland to cross before we hit forest again. Really dense. The trees run right up to the western boundary line here so we'll have plenty of cover. We're better off going in two groups." He unpacked a pair of walkie-talkies.

"Stay off them unless you have an emergency."

"Such as?" Dick asked.

Danny shrugged. "We're in bear country. This leased area here's given over to grazing. Steers, cows, bulls. There'll be moose, elk, wolf, who knows what else."

"Injuns?" Joe did a bad Groucho impression.

"Injuns." Danny nodded. "You'd better stick with me. That hair's a magnet."

I glanced across at Dick. He rubbed his shiny bald head and grinned. Despite my advice to Joe, he'd insisted on wearing his motorcycle boots whereas Dick was tricked out in a pair of hiking boots and thick walking socks. We took a backpack and headed east through the woods.

"We'll split up here," Danny said. "No point in travelling mob handed."

Dick and I turned north. Within half a minute, we'd lost sight and sound of Joe and Danny. I led the way, occasionally checking the compass hanging from my neck.

"If we see a bear," Dick said, "can we shoot it?"

"Legally?"

"Whatever."

"No."

"Can you run fast?" Dick asked.

"I don't need to run fast," I said. "Just faster than you."

We pretty much gave up talking after that. It was tougher going than I expected and we needed to watch where we stepped. The forest floor was littered with pine needles and the ground beneath our feet sounded hollow, like the skin of a drum. It was hard to see the root bowls and the burrows beneath our feet and I found myself squinting in the late afternoon light. The smells of the forest were amazing. The heady tang of pine tar filled the air, mixed with a musty smell of old earth that I found pleasing. As we moved, the sounds of the forest moved ahead of us. Squirrels chatted loudly, heralding our passing so other animals, the ones that couldn't climb trees, could make themselves scarce. Or ambush the pair of us. Shafts of sunlight streaked down from the canopy above us, dust motes, along for the ride, turning in earthbound spirals.

Before we picked up Joe and Dick, I tracked down the secretary of Cindy Palmer's condo association. I stayed with the hospital lie that she had been called to B.C. at short notice on urgent family business. I said I was Cindy's brother calling from Vancouver. The secretary, Wanda Kolinski, promised she would put out fresh food and water for Norman. I told her Norman had a cat door and that Wanda could leave the food and water on the step.

"I have two cats of my own," she said. "It won't be a problem. You think she might be gone a few days?"

"A week at most," I said. "Oh, one more thing. Cindy forgot to turn off the hot tub."

"I'm not sure I know anything about those things," she said. "But my husband's real handy. I'll take him over there with me."

I thanked her for her trouble.

"It's no trouble, you silly," she said. "We cat people must stick together."

It took us an hour and a quarter to cross the forest. We emerged onto grazing land and I looked to my right but saw no sign of Danny or Joe.

"Need a break?" I asked Dick but he shook his head. I think he was being macho.

We stepped out onto the grasslands. I could hear cattle to my left. They had sensed our presence and were lowing softly. We pushed on.

"Watch the cow patties," I called to Dick over my shoulder.

"Now you tell me."

We made good time. In less than forty more minutes we reached the woods with nary a bull in sight. We pushed ahead into another ageless green forest. This one much denser and gloomier than the first.

The trees here seemed different too. Thicker, older, as though their position closer to the prison had somehow aged them prematurely. There were more blow-downs now and we could duck under, climb over or hike around them. Each blow-down delayed us from reaching our goal. And there were fewer animal sounds too. Fewer squirrels. Fewer birds. No deer. I wondered if we were into bear territory.

"Hold up."

Dick Wyman was looking decidedly tired. His bald head shone with sweat and the blue T-shirt beneath his armpits was badly stained a darker blue. He wiped his face on the front of his T-shirt and blew a breath of air from deep within his lungs.

"You okay?" I asked and he shook his head.

"Claustrophobia," he said. "Getting a little close in here."

I looked around. The forest looked the same to me but I knew it was closing in on Dick Wyman.

"Take a break," I told him. "Sit down, get your head below your knees. Take some deep breaths, blow out slowly. That'll bring your heart rate down."

He sat against a tree, leaning against the backpack. I could hear his breathing. It was fast and ragged. I told him to slow it down otherwise he'd hyperventilate. We stayed put for another five minutes. I wondered how he had managed, inside a prison cell. He hadn't complained during the first forest crossing but this one was much denser, the trees tighter and there was less light. After a few minutes, his breathing slowed and I could tell he was gaining control. He finally looked up at me.

"Not a word, okay?"

"Sure." I nodded. "Nothing to be ashamed of, though. Lots of people get claustrophobic."

"I ain't lots'a people."

"We're halfway through," I lied.

"Liar."

"Okay, not quite halfway. You'll be okay?"

"Yeah."

"You want to lead?"

He looked up, considered this for maybe five seconds, then shook his head.

"No," he said. "I think I'm better off not knowing what's ahead."

"Okay."

I reached down and he grabbed my hand. Just as I began to pull him up, we heard a sound that bothered us.

It was loud and close and coming our way.

"The fuck's that?" he whispered but I shushed him to

silence. To my left, up ahead, I saw a shape. Maybe a hundred feet. At first, it looked almost shapeless. Just a dark mound moving over the ground towards us. Then it stopped and I saw a bear's head, his ears, his shoulders and front paws. He stood up suddenly. Even at a hundred feet, he was extraordinarily large. He swayed back and forth, his nose sniffing the air. His front claws came out an inch or two.

Then I heard another noise.

This one I knew.

Dick Wyman racked the slide of his gun, putting a bullet under the hammer.

The bear growled deeply and the air in the forest began to vibrate. The ground beneath my feet seemed to transmit that awful sound. His claws came out another inch. Then another.

"Don't!" I whispered urgently to Dick Wyman who was crouched behind me. "You'll just piss him off."

"Fuck that!" he whispered back.

The bear's jaw opened and he made a series of fast clicking sounds with his back teeth. Even at that distance, I could see the saliva strung between his teeth like Christmas lights.

Then he saw us.

He roared like a lion. Like a freight train. His whole body waved and shook. Then he dropped to all fours and, like a racehorse, covered half the distance between us in seconds.

"Move!" Dick yelled but I stood my ground and blocked his shot. I couldn't risk a shot this close to the prison. Besides, this was the bear's turf, not ours. We had no reason to kill him and, for a moment, I actually regretted being armed.

The bear rolled back up on its hind legs and threw its head up, its terrible jaws wide open. A death smile. It was giving us one last warning. We were trespassing and would pay the price. I unsnapped my holster and eased out the SIG Sauer. I wondered how close I would let it come before I fired a shot.

From the corner of my eye, I saw a movement to the left of the bear. The bear saw it too and turned to face the new intruder. It was Danny Many Guns. He walked softly and was making a noise so quiet, I was uncertain of what he was saying. Maybe nothing. Maybe he was singing, or chanting, or humming. Whatever it was, the bear watched him.

Dick Wyman had his gun arm extended to the left of my body and I reached down and pushed his arm away. I doubt he could see Danny from where he was kneeling.

The bear moved. He turned towards the new threat, the new sound moving inexorably through the forest towards him. Danny kept coming.

"What the hell?" Dick saw him at last. "He's nuts," and I must admit, the same thought had occurred to me.

The bear watched as Danny moved closer. His massive shoulders swung around and he pawed the air. Danny held something in his hand. When he squeezed, it went off with a series of muffled bangs, like a firecracker. Quieter than a gun but it startled the bear. He tossed his head back and forth but the noise did nothing to scare him off. He moved towards Danny and Danny pointed a black handgun at him. It was bigger than a regular gun. The bear took a step forward and

Danny aimed the gun at the bear. He was still chanting, a kind of singsong sound that held the bear's attention.

Then the bear decided he'd had enough.

He charged.

The handgun discharged with a soft pop. Three, four times, and each time the bear backed up, stung by the barrage of rubber bullets. Confused, the bear dropped to all fours. Then he tucked his head down and bolted through the trees towards us. I stepped back fast and knocked Dick Wyman to the ground. He told us later he could count the hairs on the bear's ass as it ran headlong between us. I don't doubt it.

I heard Dick Wyman let out a deep squeal as the bear barrelled between us.

Or maybe that was me.

Chapter Thirty-Seven

WE SET UP A FORWARD COMMAND post in a small clearing twenty feet back of the twenty-foot high wire fence topped with razor wire. Red and white signs every fifty feet warned of a potentially fatal electric shock. It was odd that the signs all faced the forest, none faced in towards the prison. I guess they assumed any escaping prisoner would figure it out. Or maybe they just didn't give a damn. From where we sat, we had a clear view of the parking lot. The parking lot was to the right of the prison. To our left, at the back of the prison on the north side, we could make out the exercise cages. Twenty-four by twenty-four foot wire boxes. Topped with razor wire. One prisoner per box. Fifteen minutes of comparative freedom, every other day. We treat animals in the zoo better than that.

The plan was simple. Since Joe and Dick both knew what Jackson Varney and Glen Pesta looked like, they would remain in the forest. Equipped with high-powered binoculars and a tripod, they would watch until either Varney or Pesta left the prison. They would then radio the car make and model to us. Since there was only one road leading from the prison, we needed to wait beyond the first junction. If he turned left, or north, he would drive past my position. If he turned right, or south, he would pass by Danny. Once we knew the direction he was headed, we could play catch-up and tail him, alternating between two cars. It really didn't matter who we followed. Once we got our hands on either Warden Varney or his son-in-law, I had no doubt about our ability to make them talk.

I unpacked both backpacks, laying out sufficient food and water for a forty-eight hour stay. They checked their guns, despite Danny's assurance that the bear was long gone. We did a brief check of the radios and I tucked a pair of spare batteries in the front pocket of one of the backpacks. Then it was time to leave.

"Good luck," Dick said as we disappeared into the forest, though we both knew he was wishing it for them more than for us.

We made good time through the woods with Danny in the lead. He seemed to flow through the trees and covered the ground like water running downhill, moving much faster than Dick had moved. We'd considered ambling along like hikers in case we were spotted but time was moving on and we needed to be in position before the warden called it a day.

The Hummer sat quietly amid the trees.

Danny had slowed the pace a quarter mile back and we'd circled the truck silently before approaching it. Danny waved me forward, comfortable that there was no one around. The Hummer was warm and safe.

As we crested the last hill on the gravel road, Danny turned onto a plain dirt road that ran down a rusty barbed wire fence line for almost a mile. We skirted a small clump of trees and came out on a blacktop road that ran through the reservation.

"So." I broke the comfortable silence that had enveloped us. "What did you say to that bear?"

Danny smiled enigmatically.

"I told him you were Goldilocks' brother, Biff, come to kick his ass."

"I could see where that would scare him." I nodded sagely but that's all he would say.

A mile further on, we came across a large building beside a gas station. There were maybe fifteen or twenty cars and trucks parked outside. Native American Indians watched us as Danny wheeled the Hummer to a stop.

I stayed put while Danny went into the building. A few curious souls wandered over to give me the eye but nobody looked too interested. A few minutes later, Danny came out and waved me over. He tossed me a set of car keys.

"Red truck." He pointed further down the building. "I'll be in the black station wagon."

The red truck started first time. On the passenger seat sat a black Stetson hat and a bright red bandana. I slipped the bandana around my neck and parked the Stetson on my head. When I checked my look in the mirror, I noticed a little wooden carving hanging from a piece of leather.

It was a black bear.

Biff Goldilocks.

Jesus H. Christ.

Chapter Thirty-Eight

WE GOT THE CALL from Joe Baker around seven-thirty that evening. I'd been parked up two miles south of the prison, facing north on a gravel road. The message was simple. Two Starboard. Which meant Glen Pesta, our number-two target, had turned right and was heading south from the prison. I fired up the truck and counted to sixty, then dropped the gear lever into drive and moved off up the road. I reached the blacktop just seconds before Pesta. I got a brief glimpse of his features as he passed in front of the truck. Darkish skin, swarthy, heavy-set with greasy black hair. I pulled out, heading in the opposite direction. I watched my rearview mirror until he was out of sight, by which time Danny was almost level, coming towards me. I stopped and powered down the window.

"Red Intrepid," I said and Danny nodded, then gunned the station wagon down the road.

I pulled a three-point turn in the road and took off after Danny. I kept the walkie-talkie turned up high. After a minute, I saw Danny in the distance. I pushed the truck harder than I should, risking a speeding ticket, then maybe jail time as I buried the needle in the red but Pesta wasn't hanging back either. I caught Danny just as the red Intrepid turned left. Danny drove past the turn and I followed the red Intrepid. I hung back, letting Pesta gain a few hundred yards ahead. At the next junction, I slowed and waited for Danny. He followed my direction and took off after Pesta. We kept this up for about eight miles, never getting closer than a few hundred yards. Finally, while I was on his tail, the Intrepid slowed and turned into a driveway. As I drove past, I glanced at the mailbox.

Pesta.

Hey Presto!

I waited for Danny a quarter mile farther down the road. Pesta's house sat on about five acres. A few trees, rolling land, a detached garage behind a two-storey house with a nice mountain view from the rear. The area was quiet. Pesta's house was flanked by similar homes, mostly five- and ten-acre parcels. There was a For Sale sign three doors down from Pesta's house on the same side. It would have to do.

"Let's do it." I spoke to Danny across the width of the truck. "I'll go in through the back. Give me —" I glanced back down the road, calculating time and distance " — fifteen minutes."

I gunned the truck around and headed back to Pesta's place. Three doors past, I turned right into the driveway of the house for sale. I parked in the drive close to the house, stepped out of the truck and made a point of looking at my watch as though I had an appointment. Nobody came to the door. I walked around the back of the house. The back was fully fenced. Five acres. About halfway down the right-hand boundary, the fence disappeared, then reappeared forty feet farther on. I walked quickly down the right-hand fence line. A dry streambed snaked across the back of several properties. We call them coolies. Maybe, come spring, there would be a trickle of water running through it but for now, it was dry and dusty. I walked down the coolie to the streambed and I was hidden from view. The barbed wire fence groaned as I pushed the bottom strand upwards and rolled beneath it. Keeping low, I followed the streambed across the next property. It levelled out before I reached Pesta's place but I kept going, running low to the ground, almost doubled over. By the time I reached Pesta's fence, my legs were cramping up. I glanced at my watch. I had eight minutes left.

As I turned to roll beneath Pesta's fence, a dog came out of nowhere. I'm not sure which one of us was more surprised. He was a black and white Border collie, a dirty blue bandana tied around his neck. He skitted sideways when he saw me and let out a yelp but he wasn't hurt, just surprised. I stayed low, whistling softly between my teeth. He cocked his head. A good sign. I reached my hand towards him, fist closed to deter him from taking it in his mouth.

Suddenly, we were friends. He bounded over, dropping one shoulder to the grass, his back legs driving him forward, his tongue flopping out, his tail beating down the tall grass. He whimpered, rolled on his back, getting his whole body into it. I rubbed his belly, his ribs, his muzzle, his thighs and his ears without moving my hand but an inch. Finally, he came to rest upside down in the grass and quieted down while I stroked him. When I moved, he moved with me.

I found a short stick in the grass and threw it for him. He was back in seconds, this time barking for more.

What the hell. I rolled beneath Pesta's fence and the dog followed. So much for stealth. I made a game of it. I threw the stick ahead of me and the dog chased it while I crawled forward as fast as I could. He brought the stick back and dropped it at my feet. As long as I kept throwing it, he agreed not to bark. I checked my watch. I had two minutes left. I whispered to the dog to sit and he sat.

I whispered him to stay and he stayed, head cocked, watching me climb quickly onto Pesta's garage roof. I crossed to the main house where an upper portion of the roof came to within eight feet of the ground. I jumped the four-foot span, then scrambled quickly up the incline to another, less steep, portion. I glanced down. The dog watched me intently. I hoped he was the only one. Pesta's back bedroom had a balcony that offered a beautiful view of the mountains. I dropped quietly from the roof and tried the double French doors. They were locked. While I went to work with my knife blade, I heard the distant chime of Pesta's doorbell. We were going on the assumption that Glen Pesta did not know Danny Many Guns. Even if he did, he'd hardly be expecting Danny to show up on his doorstep. Danny would pretend to be interested in buying the place three doors down and was worried about the well. Had Pesta had any problems with his water supply?

The door gave under my knife blade. I eased it open and stepped into Glen Pesta's bedroom. Queen size bed, two pillows, night tables, chest of drawers, walk-in closet, en suite bathroom. A woman's housecoat hung from the back of the bedroom door. I tiptoed across the room, eased the door open a crack. I could hear a woman's voice below. The hallway was wide, the front entrance visible through the light oak railings. I chanced a peek.

I saw a woman.

And I saw Danny.

I stepped back out of sight. I knew that Danny had seen me. I slid down the hall soundlessly and pushed open a bedroom door. A child's room. I stuck my head inside. The bed was made. Stuffed toys, a pink Disney border. A girl's room, maybe four years old. The next bedroom was vacant. Furnished with an unused air. The guest room.

There was another room at the opposite end of the hall.

I should have checked it first.

As I stepped back out into the hall, Glen Pesta was waiting for me, an evil-looking shotgun levelled straight at my face.

Chapter Thirty-Nine

"GLEN?" The woman called from down below. "Glen!"

Pesta ignored her. He put his fingers to his lips. Then described a circle. He wanted me to turn around.

I didn't like what was coming.

"We're not alone." I spoke loudly. "The police have your place surrounded."

His finger twitched a quarter inch. I flinched but kept my hands raised and turned around. I was expecting a blow to the head and I lowered my hands a little to take the brunt of it. But he had something else in mind. He drove the shotgun stock deep into my left kidney. The pain was excruciating. I dropped to my knees. I tried to warn Danny that he had a shotgun but nothing came out. Nothing at all. He'd driven every last ounce of breath from my body. Then he went for the head shot, cracking me hard across the side of my skull with the stock. I felt my head implode, then mercifully, nothing at all.

I didn't even hear Danny leave.

Chapter Forty

SOMEONE WAS KICKING ME. Not hard but insistent. Kick. Pause. Kick. Pause. I tried to roll away but they followed. Kick. Kick. Kick. No pauses now. It was extremely uncomfortable and my head hurt like a son of a bitch. I was lying on a concrete floor. My hands were held behind my back. Handcuffs, some part of my brain told me. Some part that didn't ache. So only a small part. A deep pain riddled my lower back.

"Up," Kicker said. "Get up."

I turned over, onto my knees. Christ. Someone had ripped out a major organ. They'd removed one of my kidneys but I couldn't tell which one. Maybe both. My stomach turned over and I retched but nothing came out.

"Get him up."

The Kicker wasn't alone.

Hands grabbed me, dragged me upright, then turned and slammed me into a chair. The chair didn't move. It was bolted to the floor. Chairs bolted to the floor were never a good sign. I chanced a look up. There were two of them in the room with me. The room looked strange. It had concrete walls. I couldn't see any windows.

Another bad sign.

Name, rank and serial number.

"Look at me."

I wasn't sure which one of them spoke. I glanced back up. Glen Pesta stepped back. Warden Jackson Varney leaned forward, his dark eyes locked on my face. He was a big man. Gone a bit to fat over the years but still big. Powerful shoulders, short arms, thick biceps. His head disappeared into his neck — a large head and a thick neck. Bad skin as a youth, pockmarks the size of dimes. His hair was cut short, flecked through with grey. His pupils were big. Dark pools that reflected nothing back at you. The eyes of a dead fish.

A shark.

"Hey, Jacko." I smiled a crinkly smile and he hit me hard with the flat of his hand. The blow blew me right out of the chair.

They played this game where Pesta would slam me into the chair and Varney would slam me back out. I lost count but it didn't matter because nobody was keeping score. But they kept it even. First the right side of my face. Then the left. Jacko. An equal opportunity slapper.

They kept it up for what seemed like hours. I do believe I passed out a few times but never for very long. Varney finally grew tired of it but that was long after I'd grown tired of it myself. He reached out and laid his hands on my shoulders. I twitched, expecting a slap, and he snorted. Not with humour. Just derision.

"Who'd you tell?" His voice sounded like it was coming from a different part of the room. I wondered if he'd detached my eardrums. Can they do that?

"Everybody. Nobody." I slurred so badly, I wasn't sure they could understand me. "Tell who what?"

I think there was drool running down my chin. Or maybe blood. My face felt numb from all the slapping. Yet it stung like crazy. What a crazy world.

"Who's the Indian," Varney said.

Words slurred their way out the side of my mouth.

"What'd he say?"

"Who knows?" Pesta shrugged.

"Goddamn it!" Varney hit me another hard crack.

I felt myself sliding off the chair.

"Leave him," Varney growled.

I hit the floor and lay there like a crumpled bag of rags. I wondered if the Border collie was still waiting round the back of Pesta's house for me. Then I stopped thinking for a long time.

When I woke up the next time, I was still on the floor. My head still hurt, my kidneys still felt like they were missing and my cheeks glowed an unhealthy, nuclear meltdown red. I tried to scratch myself but my hands were still cuffed.

It sucked.

I went back to sleep but not for long. Someone threw a bucket of cold water over me. This time, I came around fully alert. Wide-awake and in touch with all my senses. Rough hands hauled me back into the chair. This time, they duct taped me to it. Duct tape. That's probably not a good thing either. I tried to hold my extremities away from my body while they wrapped the duct tape around me. Like that would make a difference.

Glen Pesta admired his handiwork. At least, he hadn't taped my mouth shut.

"You think the cops don't know?" I said.

"Know what?"

"About your little scam."

Pesta looked around the room.

"I see no cops."

"Oh, they know all right." But even I didn't sound convinced.

Varney moved back into my field of vision. He had something in his hand but his hand was so damned big, I couldn't really tell what he was holding. He reached back and I heard the sound of a chair scrape across the concrete floor. He sat in it backwards, the way kids do when they pretend they're on a horse.

"You ever been to Mexico?" he asked me, trying for a conversational tone.

"Yeah."

"Ever been in a Mexican prison?" he asked.

"No."

"Interesting places, Mexican prisons."

He raised his hand to his face and put something in his mouth, tipped it up and swallowed. It looked like he might be holding a bottle.

"If you say so."

"I was down there seven, eight years back. When they was having all them riots. You remember that?"

"Yes."

He took another swig from the bottle.

"It was a teaching seminar. Teaching the Federales about prison security." He took another slow swig. "A riot broke out. The local warden was on the seminar with me. He got a phone call. Invited a few of us to tag along. Said we might learn something about discipline." He took another swig from the bottle and this time he let me see what it was.

Somewhere, deep in the darkest corners of my brain, a little bell began to toll.

A warning bell.

He was swigging from a Coke bottle.

Things go better with Coca-Cola.

Except when you're duct taped to a metal chair, bolted to a concrete floor with your hands locked behind your back. Then things don't go better with Coke. Especially in Mexican prisons. I'd heard about that particular torture. I knew what was coming and I didn't like it at all.

Not one bit.

"When we reached the prison, the riot was in full swing. They'd knifed two guards, left their bodies out in the open. They were still alive. Nobody felt like going in to get them out. The prisoners set fire to their mattresses. They ripped the toilets off the wall and threw them over the walkways. They gang-raped the padres they didn't like. Tied them with sheets to the cells bars and raped them over and over again. Full-scale riot. Never seen anything like it. Then the warden made a phone call. Just one. That's all it needed. He called the local bottler. Ordered a case of Coca-Cola. In bottles. Just like this."

He held his hand open. The red and white logo looked incongruous in his large, rough hand. He took another slow swig.

"Where's Cindy?" I said.

"Who've you told?"

"Where's Lindsay?"

"Who's your Injun friend?"

"Let the ladies go. Then I'll tell you."

He leaned forward, his face inches from mine. His breath smelled sweet from the cola.

"Don't take me for a cunt," he said, cold as ice. "You never want to do that."

"Likewise." I held his glare until even Pesta got uncomfortable.

"Jacko," Pesta said. "Let's move this along, okay?"

Jacko never looked away. He never blinked, he just continued with his terrible story, speaking it right into my face, his words full of spittle that went right from his mouth into mine.

"They delivered the Coca-Cola in a big truck. Just wheeled it right into that yard. And do you know what happened when those cons saw that Coca-Cola truck? Those murderers, rapists, rock hard men every last one of them. Do you know what they did? They ran. They ran and hid. They ran and hid and shook with fear and they pissed themselves. And they cried. When the guards walked in and handpicked twenty-four for discipline, they cried. Grown men, howled like babies."

I saw Glen Pesta out the corner of my eye as he stepped behind me.

"Do you know why?"

I might have nodded my head but I had no chance. Pesta grabbed me from behind. He locked my head in a grip like a vise. And Jacko, with his thumb over the mouth of the bottle, shook it gently, like it was no big deal. When he shook it a little harder, the corners of his mouth curled up like a feral dog that's discovered it likes to kill things.

"Let me give you a taste," he said. And that's when the pain really started.

Chapter Forty-One

I HAVE LOST TRACK OF TIME. I have lost track of my senses. I have lost track of everything except the pain. I can no longer remember what it is I must do to stop the terrible, raging hurt that has turned my world inside out. And that makes it all the worse. I see his thumb cover the mouth of the bottle, see his hand shake as he masturbates the Coke bottle, infuriating the millions of tiny bubbles trapped inside. The pressure builds. The only relief is when he slides his thumb from the opening. But their relief is my misery for the mouth of the bottle is jammed up inside my nostril and I am powerless to prevent what is about to happen. I'm tied and taped and locked in place and now the pressure inside the bottle is released as he slides his thumb away and the gaseous, foaming, pressurized mass rushes to fill every cavity inside my head.

The pain instantly overwhelms me. I have never experienced anything like it in my life. It fills my nostrils, my throat, my ears, it pours out of my mouth and pours down into my lungs. It expands my sinus cavities beyond anything they were ever designed to handle. My body bucks and writhes against the restraints and liquid pain fills my being. I would sell my mother's eyes if they would stop. I would take them out of her eye sockets with a metal spoon and eat them raw if they would only stop. The pressure is beyond anything a human could ever endure. They tire of one nostril and infiltrate the other.

I pass out.

Again.

And again.

And again.

Chapter Forty-Two

IT IS DARK.

Everything inside my body has become detached. Someone once said all pain is referred pain, except a direct blow. All other pain is referred. Pain is the shoreline, where the sea washes up on the sand. That's where the pain is felt. But it starts miles out at sea. It starts in an undercurrent, a riptide, a maelstrom deep in the ocean. It's transmitted to shore but there's no point treating the shoreline. You need to go deep, then deeper, then deeper still. But no matter how deep I go, I cannot find where this pain begins. Or ends. This pain will last forever.

It is still dark.

I have never known such misery.

Chapter Forty-Three

CINDY IS LOOKING AT ME.

I blink back tears of relief.

"Cindy?" A croak, a voice I don't recognize. I try again. "Babe?"

"Eddie."

Her voice is soft. The voice of an angel. She speaks to me again but I cannot understand her words. Someone is pushing a cloth in her face, covering her mouth, covering the promise of her lips. She tries to scream but it's all too late.

For both of us.

And for Lindsay too.

The room is different. It's still a concrete room but there is no chair. Only me and Cindy and Lindsay.

And Jacko the Wacko and Glen Pesta.

Hey Presto.

And something else.

Something bolted to the floor.

I realize what it is.

And what they intend to do to us.

I try to yell, to tell Cindy and Lindsay to run but Pesta has a rag down my throat. I catch a glimpse of Lindsay's face. She is beyond terror. I never got a chance to know her. I try to know her with my eyes. They push me roughly to the floor.

I feel the cold steel plates of the paint shaker as they tighten them around my head. I try to console myself that at least I'm going first but that's no consolation. The screw thread turns beneath me, catching loose strands of hair. It tears them out. The metal plates tighten along the sides of my head, overlapping along my cheekbones. The pressure increases. My head is jammed. I cannot move.

I lie, face-up, bound hand and foot. Every part of my being aches. It is a great, all-consuming pain. I am fatigued beyond belief and yet still I struggle, still I try to break free. Above me, Jackson Varney bends forward until his face is just inches from mine. His great ugly gash of a mouth splits apart in what he believes is a smile.

"You lose." He speaks to me and somewhere behind my head I sense the turning of a switch and for a brief split-second I hear the terrible hum of an electric motor that translates to a violence I cannot imagine. The warden's face morphs from one face into a million, their outlines blur and melt, collide and reform as the machine begins to shake every molecule that is me, every cell that knows I am Eddie Dancer, every atom, every synapse, every particle of my soul. It shakes the delicate chemicals that bring me joy and ela-tion and fear and thrilling adventure and mixes them all into one jellified mass of nothing that will resemble a brain or a mind or anything human from this point forward. My

brain morphs into a vegetable.
And darkness descends.
Then all grows quiet.

Chapter Forty-Four

DANNY MANY GUNS FOLLOWED Eddie Dancer in the red truck. When Eddie turned up the drive of the house for sale, Danny began timing him. He waited on the blacktop, keeping an eye out for Eddie, eventually spotting him close to the back of Pesta's house, followed by a dog.

Danny waited, giving Eddie time to case the back of Pesta's house. When fifteen minutes had passed, Danny drove up Pesta's drive and pulled up close to the front door. He did a three-point turn and parked facing the road. He stepped out, walked quickly to the front door and rang the bell. He heard the bell chime through the house and wondered if Eddie could hear it. A moment later, the door opened and a woman in her mid-thirties peered out at him.

"Excuse me." Danny shuffled his feet. "I'm sorry to bother you. I'm thinking of making an offer for the house up the road." he pointed in the direction of the house.

"The Pruitts'?" she said.

"Yes. I wonder if your husband would mind answering a couple of questions about the wells around here."

"Well, let's ask him." She stepped aside. "Come in."

Danny stepped into the front hall. He scanned the upper level quickly. He saw Eddie Dancer through the oak railings.

"I'm not sure where he went," the woman said. "Glen?" She waited a moment then called him again. "Glen!"

Danny saw a movement upstairs. He knew it wasn't Eddie, he'd gone the other way. He heard Eddie's voice, clear and distinct.

"We are not alone."

Danny stepped back quickly, getting behind Glen Pesta's wife.

He heard a sound. A thump. Then a man stepped into his field of vision for a brief moment and Danny saw the shotgun aimed at him. It took a split second to consider his options. He could extend his gun arm and take Glen Pesta's wife hostage. But Glen Pesta had Eddie. And they still had Cindy and her daughter. Danny doubted one for three would give him much bargaining power.

He could try and take Glen Pesta out of the play. He knew he was fast enough but then what? They still needed to get Cindy and Lindsay back.

His only other option was to leave. And live to fight another day. Knowing Eddie had a partner, Pesta wouldn't do anything too stupid. Danny pushed Pesta's wife to block the shot and stepped back quickly. When Glen Pesta's wife turned around, Danny had disappeared.

He drove fast down the drive, keeping low in the seat. He hit the blacktop and accelerated hard until he was no longer in sight of the house, his mind racing. He knew Glen

Pesta would either leave the house or someone would come for him. Danny slowed, pulled a U-turn and drove slowly back up the road until he could see the front entrance of Pesta's property. The driveway across the road was concealed behind a cluster of trees. Danny backed in, reversed up twenty feet, shielded by the undergrowth. It worked both ways. He couldn't be seen from the road nor the house.

Ten minutes later, he watched Glen Pesta gunning his red Intrepid out onto the blacktop. He knew that Eddie was in the trunk. The tires squealed as Pesta peeled rubber. Danny eased down the driveway. His timing needed to be perfect. He gunned the motor, his foot hard on the brake. As Pesta's Intrepid drew almost level with the driveway, Danny came off the brake. Timed right, he planned to clip the front end of Pesta's car, pushing him off the road.

And it would have worked.

His timing was perfect.

But the black and white Border collie with the dirty blue bandana ran across the end of the drive as Danny released the brake. His instincts betrayed him and he hit the brakes, jamming the car into the tree line to avoid killing the dog.

Pesta was a mile down the road before Danny got the wagon free of the undergrowth. He wasn't hard to follow because Danny knew he was headed back to the prison. When Pesta reached the parking lot, there were several guards waiting for him. Pesta opened the trunk lid and Danny watched from a distance as they lifted Eddie out. They half-carried, half-dragged him into Barbary Prison.

Danny keyed the walkie-talkie and Joe Baker answered.

"Did you see that?"

"Who the fuck was it?" Joe said.

"Eddie."

"Aw, shit!"

"Go! South! Fifteen minutes!"

Danny backed up, turned and drove away from the Barbary Prison complex.

Joe Baker and Dick Wyman threw their belongings into the backpacks and crashed noisily through the woods, heading due south.

"We see another bear," Joe said, "I'm gonna shoot it."

Dick didn't say anything but Joe noticed he, too, travelled with his gun out. In fifteen minutes, they emerged, hot and tired, beside the east-west road, well south of the prison. Danny was waiting for them a hundred yards to the west.

"What happened?" Joe demanded.

"Things went sour," Danny said and told them what he knew.

"Now what?" Joe said.

"Eddie had a plan," Danny told him.

"I'm sure he did." Joe was less than enthused.

When Danny told them, Joe shook his head in disbelief.

"Never in a month of fuckin' Sundays, Tonto."

"Dick?" Danny watched him in the rearview mirror.

"Don't ask me." Dick shook his head. "Sounds like a good way to get your head blown off."

"Are you in or out?"

"Aw, fuck." Dick shook his head. "Sue-Ann'll kill me."

"Is that a yes?"

"Yeah." Sullen.

"Joe?"

"I'm here ain't I?"

"Appreciate it," Danny said.

"Whatever," Joe said and turned away, looking out the window the rest of the way into the city.

Danny wondered if there would be anyone left alive by morning.

Chapter Forty-Five

DANNY DROVE THE STATION WAGON back downtown, switching lanes rapidly to gain every advantage on the way to his apartment. He drove past his apartment building twice, telling Joe and Dick to keep their eye out for anything suspicious.

"You think they're staking you out?"

"I don't think they know who I am. Yet. I just can't take that chance right now."

"You think Eddie's gonna tell them anything?"

"It's not a question of what he'll tell them. It's a question of when. Everyone talks eventually."

Danny pulled into his parking stall and the three of them walked quickly into the building. Once inside, they rode the elevator two floors above Danny's. He told Joe to keep his finger on the Door Open button.

"If anyone wants to use the elevator, you have my permission to shoot them."

"Never need permission," Joe said but Danny was gone.

He backtracked to the stairwell, his hand resting on

the gun at his waist. The east stairwell was empty. He ran quickly down two levels until he was satisfied there was no one hiding in wait for him. He did the same in the west stairwell and came up empty again.

He ran back up stairs and joined Joe and Dick in the waiting elevator. He hit the button for his own floor. They rode the two floors in silence. When the elevator stopped, Danny told them to wait.

He walked quickly down the hallway and pressed his ear against the door, out of sight of the spy hole. He heard nothing. He slid the key into the lock and turned it, hearing the well-oiled tumblers aligning inside. Then he pushed the door open to the wall and listened, then waved Dick and Joe down the hallway. Three armed men. They all moved cautiously through Danny's immaculate apartment.

The place was empty.

Now they looked for something smaller. Danny knew what he was looking for but he didn't know where it was. He hoped to God Eddie didn't have it on him.

"This your place?" Joe gave a low whistle.

"Yes."

"What'd you do? Rob a fuckin' bank?"

"I work," Danny said and shot Joe Baker a look that shut him up. "You know what we're looking for?"

"What are we, dumb fucks?" Joe moved ahead, scanning the living room for the phone book that Eddie had taken from Len and Doug's place.

They searched the whole place. A thorough search of Eddie's room proved fruitless. While Dick searched the kitchen, Joe searched the living room. Danny was beginning to lose hope. The bathroom yielded nothing, neither did the study. What was Eddie wearing that day? Danny searched Eddie's clothes in the wash hamper but found nothing. Had he hidden it? Had he realized its importance and found a hiding place?

Danny joined the others in the living room.

"Maybe he took it with him," Dick said. "Maybe it's in the car. Or the Hummer."

"Shit." Joe Baker shook his head. "Dumb fuckin' idea to begin with, you ask me."

He sat down in Danny's leather armchair. Something poked him in the butt. He reached down and pulled out the fanny pack Eddie had worn to go jogging.

"A purse? What sort of fairy wears a fuckin' purse?" He tossed it aside and Danny caught it.

Inside, he found the phone book they'd been looking for.

Joe Baker stood up. "Let's get outa here. This fuckin' place gives me the willies."

Danny took a last look around before he locked the door.

He knew he might not be back.

Chapter Forty-Six

THEY COMMANDEERED A CORNER BOOTH at Ralph's Place on Seventh Avenue. A surly waitress named Margo took their order. Danny ordered a glass of water and went to work on Len and Doug's address book.

He began with the *As*. There were two names with the letter B in a circle. The first was Al Greenwood, the second Andy Aubee. Danny punched in the first number.

No answer.

He tried Andy Aubee.

After a few seconds, the phone was answered.

"Yeah?" A dark, suspicious voice.

"Andy?"

"Who?"

"I'm looking for Andy Aubee."

"You got the wrong number."

"I don't think I do," Danny said.

"I don't give a shit."

Joe Baker reached over and took the phone out of Danny's hand.

"Orb, you fuck. What's up, man?"

"Who's that?"

"S'Joe Baker. Now shut the fuck up and listen to the man. He's gonna make you a deal."

Joe handed the cell phone back to Danny.

"Hello?"

"What you want?"

"I've a job for you."

"I gotta job."

"Not anymore. Jacko laid you off."

"So? You think I can't get another fuckin' job?"

"Not one that pays like this."

"What's the job?"

When Danny told him, the phone went silent.

"You're a fuckin' head case."

"We can do this," Danny told him.

"How much you talking?"

"Your share. It's your money, after all. What's that? Six figures, maybe more?"

"The fuck you smokin'?"

"You want a shot, eight o'clock tonight, North Hill Mall parking lot, across from the cinema."

Danny hung up.

He worked his way through Len's phone book. He got a lot of wrong numbers but slowly, painstakingly, the word went out. When he finished calling everyone with a circled B in the book, he paid the tab and the three of them drove out to the North Hill Mall just before eight o'clock. They knew the risk. Any one of Jacko's ex-cons could turn them in but Danny was banking on them showing up just to hear the plan. He counted on them wanting to take a run at Jackson Varney, to even up the score and get their hands on the mother lode they knew he had stashed away.

Danny drove slowly past the spot. There was nobody there.

"Let me out," Joe said.

Danny stopped the car and Joe stepped out.

"Git." Joe waved him away.

It didn't take long. An older model black Camaro rumbled past. Joe nodded and the driver backed up. They talked for a minute and the driver found a parking space. As the Camaro pulled ahead, an old Thunderbird took its place. Over the next fifteen minutes, fourteen cars glided by, each stopping to talk briefly with Joe Baker. Some he knew, others he knew by reputation. Those he didn't know, he showed them his snake and dagger tattoo. Five cars left. That left nine. An even dozen counting Danny, Dick and Joe Baker.

It would have to do.

Chapter Forty-Seven

FROM HIS CONVERSATION with Phillip P. Wilson, Danny knew the Barbary employed about one hundred and twenty prison guards. They worked a three-shift rotation. Each new day began at six a.m. and each shift ran for eight hours. The busiest shifts ran from six-to-two and two-to-ten. The quietest ran from ten at night until six the next morning. The night shift got by with less than a dozen guards.

Danny doubled up his crew, two per car. He didn't need a dozen cars blocking the highway. He chose those with the largest trunk space. They synchronized their watches and their dashboard clocks. Those without a watch rode with those that had one. They were to rendezvous at a spot two miles from the Prison at nine-twenty that evening.

"Don't be late." He pulled away from the group, Dick Wyman along with him.

"I'm having second thoughts," Dick told him and Danny laughed.

"Join the club."

They rode in silence for a while but Dick's nerves were

getting the better of him.

"This is crazy" he said, breaking the silence. "We're gonna break into a maximum security prison."

"Easier than breaking out," Danny said.

"Those guards are trained to shoot," Dick said. "Mass density training. They ain't gonna shoot you in the arm. They'll go for the body shot."

"Nobody's going to get shot. They have no idea we're coming. Just relax."

"Easy for you to say."

"You want out?" Danny slowed the car.

"Hell, no." Dick was offended. "I gave you my word, dammit. That means something to me."

"Me, too."

"But that don't stop me from complaining," Dick said. "It helps blow off steam. I'll be fine. You worry about your own ass."

Danny pulled onto a service road leading to a series of late-night stores. Petlands, Staples, Co-op and Home Depot.

"We need some stuff from the hardware store," Danny said and Dick walked in with him.

They bought a large, yellow-handled sledgehammer, three six-foot long crowbars, a flashlight and a roll of duct tape.

"That's all?"

"That's all the plan calls for," Danny said.

"Jesus." Dick shook his head. "We're screwed."

They arrived twelve minutes ahead of schedule. Danny pulled over, onto the grass, careful not to roll the station wagon into the ditch. The one-road-in, one-road-out lay-out of the prison was designed to make a prison break that' much harder. A mile-long road with no side roads and a north-south T-junction meant the authorities knew which direction an escaping prisoner was headed. But it worked both ways. People coming to the prison would be travel-ling either northbound or southbound before turning west. Danny's plan was to catch them off guard before they reached the westbound highway.

Two of the cars were a few minutes late. Danny had all but given up on them when they cruised to a halt.

"Follow those two, that way" He pointed north. "You —" he turned to the other late arrival "— stay with my group."

"What's the plan?" the passenger asked.

"You know the plan."

"I mean, if anything goes wrong?"

"Stick with the plan," Danny told him.

"I mean, really goes wrong?"

"It won't."

By nine-forty, all six cars were in place. Danny parked the station wagon on the north-south country road and popped the hood. He waved the second car past. The driver stopped, then backed up, ramming Danny's station wagon on its left front fender. Glass shattered and a jet of steam sprayed from the radiator. The third car squeezed past the wreckage and pulled up twenty yards ahead. It looked like a bad accident.

"You —" Danny pointed to the man nearest to him "— get down on the road!"

The man rolled around on the blacktop, moaning.

"Je-sus," someone said. "Gimme a break," but Danny wasn't bothered. This wasn't a plan that would be scuttled by bad acting.

The rest of the team hunkered down in the ditches, out of sight of the road. Only Danny and the injured man rolling in the road remained in full view.

They were just in time.

Chapter Forty-Eight

DARYL KURTZ HAD BEEN A PRISON-GUARD most of his adult life. At fifty-five, he'd seen it all. Or thought he had. He drove a blue Dodge Caravan. He had four grandchildren and his back seat was littered with children's car seats and candy wrappers. Riding with him was Normie Quinn, a rookie prison guard half his age. Normie's car was in the shop and he was grateful for the ride. He'd been late once this month already. He couldn't afford another reprimand. At first glance, they could have passed for cops. The Barbary favoured two-tone blue for their dress code. They were making small talk when Daryl noticed the accident up ahead.

"What the heck." He pulled up behind the station wagon. Both men climbed out and ran towards Danny who was kneeling over a man lying moaning in the road. "You need a hand there, fellah?"

Danny turned sharply, his gun centred on Daryl Kurtz's forehead

"Over there, both of you." Danny waved them over to the front of the station wagon where shadows emerged from the ditch. "Strip," he told them, "or you'll both be shot."

Neither man was armed. The guards at the Barbary did not pick up their weapons until their shift started. The federal government did not see the point in paying for more weapons than were actually required.

Daryl Kurtz had been around prisoners all his life. He knew when a fight was about to break out. He knew when a prisoner had nothing left to lose and he knew which ones were dangerous and which ones were more so. He also knew when an ex-con held a gun to your head, it was imperative you do what you're told. Normie, on the other hand, wanted to show how brave and strong and young and foolish he was.

He tried to run back to the Dodge and might have made it but Dick Wyman was waiting for him. He clotheslined him just as Normie made the turn across the front of the Dodge. He went down in a heap, gagging and coughing but still fighting. His shirt got ripped and he didn't settle down until somebody clipped him upside the head. They locked Daryl Kurtz and Normie Quinn in the trunk of the second car.

Three more cars arrived in quick succession, five more guards in all. Unarmed, they were no match for the ex-cons who roughed up a few of them for past transgressions.

By nine-fifty Danny and the five ex-cons in his team wore the two-tone blue slacks and shirts of the Barbary Prison guards. Joe Baker had the other group under control. Everything had gone according to plan.

They jammed the road with surplus vehicles, blocking anyone else from getting through.

"Let's roll!" Danny led the way as they drove quickly to the T-junction. From there they drove in a staggered convoy up the mile-long road towards Barbary Prison, keeping to the speed limit. Keeping below the radar.

Chapter Forty-Nine

DICK WYMAN WAS RIDING with Danny and Andy Aubee, the man Joe Baker called Orb. Orb said the hardest part would be getting in through the second of the two main gates. Each gate was twenty feet tall, topped with razor wire. The inner gate could not be opened until the outer gate had closed. By the time they reached the inner gate, they would be close enough for the two gate guards to ID them.

However, it wasn't just the prison guards who operated on the eight-hour triple-shift system. Almost everyone did. The cooks, the cleaners, the maintenance crew. Orb told Danny to pull up, nose first, facing the gates. From there, they could see beyond the gates and into the long narrow corridor that connected the gates to the rest of the prison. It didn't take long before they spotted a group of six civilians heading towards them down the corridor.

"Easy," Danny said and Dick took his hand back off the door handle.

They waited until the group was halfway along the corridor before they opened the car doors.

"Show time." Orb grinned and Danny and Dick followed his lead. Danny wore a baseball cap low across his brow to conceal his features. As they approached the outer gate, one of the gate guards keyed the open switch. The big gate slid silently open and the three of them stepped through. By now, the civilians were approaching the inner gate. From the gatehouse, the guard saw the three arriving guards pick up the pace. He assumed they were being helpful, arriving at the inner gate at the same time as the civilian group. When the outer gate closed, the green light on his console lit up and he keyed the inner gate to open so the civilians and the guards could pass through the inner gate simultaneously. Technically, it was against regulations. The civilian group leaving the prison were supposed to wait until the guards had entered, the gate had closed and then re-opened before they crossed over. But nobody followed that rule on a shift change. The gate guards wanted to go home, too.

By the time the gate guards realized their mistake, it was too late to do anything about it.

"Move back." Danny spoke quietly.

It was three on two and neither of the gate guards had a chance to draw their weapon. They were handcuffed together, gagged and forced to lay face down on the floor.

Orb stayed on the gate while Dick and Danny moved ahead. The rest of the team was already converging quickly on the outer gate, which remained open after the civilians had passed through. Joe Baker detoured over to Danny's station wagon and hefted the yellow sledgehammer and the six-foot iron crowbars, along with the flashlight. Dick had taped the three bars together with the roll of duct tape.

"Take this." Joe handed the bars to Gary Paxton, another ex-con. "Follow me."

The Barbary Prison, considered a Super-Prison (an American term), was anything but. It was built to be escape-proof. There were no overhead power cables, phone cables or any other data cables coming into the prison. Everything came in underground to make it near impossible to cut any cables from the outside. The individual cell door locks and cellblock door locks were keyless. They required a data card to open and close them. Almost everything was electronic and computer controlled. The cells were built to minimize the noise level so noisy prisoners didn't disturb the guards. Lock-down was nine-thirty in the evening. Wake-up was six-thirty in the morning.

Danny's most pressing problem was the changing of the guard. The fifty or so armed guards from the two-to-ten shift were gathered in the Armory, signing over their weapons and ammunition. The Armory was located on the left side of the narrow corridor.

"Now what?" Dick asked as the two of them moved quickly down the corridor.

"Get ready," Danny said.

The Armory door was clearly marked. It was a heavy metal door with a nine-by-nine-inch heavy plate-glass window embedded in the upper section. The glass was cross-hatched with chicken wire. There was an electronic lock on the door with a ten-number keypad. The number was changed daily to minimize the risk of prison rioters getting hold of the weaponry. The door opened inwards and had a deep, heavy metal handle on each side. The handles were roughly ten inches long and stood three inches proud of the door. More than enough room for the modified crowbars.

Joe Baker moved up with Gary Paxton on his heels. The two men stayed below the level of the window. Joe guided the crowbars into the space created by the handle. It was like threading an enormous needle. Paxton pushed the bars into place. They overlapped the Armory door by over a foot either side. It would take a tank to tear the door open. Joe left Paxton in charge of guarding the crowbars.

Danny, Dick and Joe Baker crossed the corridor to a door on the far right marked Maintenance. If anyone had seen them through the thick glass, he would assume they were part of the guard change. The rest of the ex-cons moved quickly down the corridor.

The maintenance door was locked. It wasn't equipped with a key card lock but an old-fashioned set of tumblers, because outside maintenance workers needed access to this room and giving them an electronic key card was considered a security risk.

"You're up," Danny told Dick.

Dick Wyman dropped to one knee. He took a slim leather pouch from his inside pocket and unwrapped it quickly, then peered into the lock with a narrow penlight. He picked two thin metal bars, one with a tight hook on the end, the other like a short Allen key. It took him thirty-seven seconds to pick the lock.

When Dick popped the door open, Danny and Joe Baker followed him into the maintenance room.

The room was painted bright white. A row of silent gas furnaces stood along the right-hand wall. Several huge hot-water tanks stood at the far end. A series of electrical boxes was mounted along the left-hand wall. Danny counted eight in total. Each box had a grey metal cover, locked securely in place. Behind each panel, Danny knew, were rows of fuses. Each fuse would be marked to show what part of the system it controlled. Although each box was secured to the concrete wall, the boxes looked as if they were balanced on a thick plastic pipe that came up through the floor to the underside of each box. Each pipe passed through a main switch. It was a building code requirement. The main switch had to be separate from the box itself. Each main switch cover was locked with a padlock. Danny turned to Joe Baker.

"Go," he said.

Joe stood with his feet apart. He hefted the sledgehammer in his big, rough hands, then brought it down hard on the first padlock. It took three blows to shatter the lock. He moved quickly to the next as Danny opened the buckled door wide enough to reach the main switch. He shut off the power to the first box.

Dick and Danny followed Joe Baker down the row, turning off each box as Joe blew the locks apart. When Danny turned off the fifth box, the room lights went out.

"Flashlight!" Danny called and Dick angled the beam to help Joe finish up. When he finished, he tossed the heavy sledgehammer across the room. He hadn't even broken a sweat.

"Lock the door," Danny told Dick. "Nobody gets in. I'll come back and get you when we're done."

They stepped back out into the corridor. Someone was hammering on the door of the Armory.

From the inside.

With the power out, the locks couldn't be opened. Even if the guards could override the lock, the crowbar would keep them prisoners in their own jail. The back-up generators provided emergency lighting only and the corridor was bathed in a dim glow.

Danny and the ex-cons ran down the narrow corridor. There was a series of doors right and left but he ignored them. At the end of the corridor, the double doors stood closed.

"It's okay," an ex-con told him. "We're still in the common area."

He pushed the release bar and the left-hand door swung inward. They were on the lower level of the three-tiered building. Heavy cage wire separated the three levels and a metal staircase ran up from a central aisle. Along the walls, heavy concrete rooms housed the prison population. The prisoners knew something was wrong. As thick as the walls were, Danny could hear them banging and complaining. Several guards ran along the upper tier.

Danny turned quickly to the ex-cons. "Go and get what you came for," Danny said. "I'll find Eddie."

The men began running down the central aisle. Danny was undecided which way to go.

He closed his eyes and asked his Spirit Guide for help.

Chapter Fifty

WHEN THE LIGHTS WENT OUT, Jackson Varney lost his bearings for a moment. The windowless room was plunged into total darkness. It was an isolation cell, designed to create the most miserable conditions a human being could endure. Soundproof, it created sensory deprivation from the outset. The record was eight days. After that, the mind went into meltdown. The guards referred to eight-day isolation survivors as "deep fried." For good reason. Jackson turned hurriedly and groped for the door. He knew if the lights went out, there was a problem with the power and that meant a problem with the door locks. He found the door handle and wrenched the door wide open a split second before Danny Many Guns threw the next switch, two hundred yards away.

"Christ! That was close!" Jacko said.

"What the hell!" Glen Pesta almost tripped over Eddie Dancer lying prone on the floor of the cell.

"The damn power's out," Jacko said. "I just got the door open in time."

"Fuck!"

A row of dim red lights illuminated the catwalk outside the cell. Planning for power outages, the security company responsible for Barbary Prison had strongly recommended not having a back-up generator for the electronic locks. If the power went down due to an attempted prison break, the last thing you wanted was a few hundred stir-crazy prisoners on the loose. The decision was unanimous. There was no back-up generator for the power locks, only for the emergency lighting.

"Go see what the hell's happening," Jacko barked and Glen Pesta eased his way across the cell.

Pesta unsnapped the leather sap from his belt and slid his government-issue handgun from its holster. At the door, he reached down and pulled off one of Eddie's shoes to use as a doorstop. He turned to Cindy Palmer and her daughter.

"I'll be back," he said. "Then it's your turn."

Cindy grabbed Lindsay just as her daughter let out a terrified scream.

Chapter Fifty-One

DANNY MANY GUNS TURNED TO THE RIGHT, in the direction of a scream. It was a young girl's scream, high-pitched and terrifying. He moved away from the rail. His feet seemed to glide across the floor. The corridor ahead resembled an underground tunnel. Thin red light leaked from the ceiling overhead. Danny moved quickly, his fingertips brushing the wall to his right. The lighting was so poor, he could barely see ten feet down the corridor. The corridor made a sharp right turn. He moved faster now, silent and skilful, bathed in red light like an avenging spirit.

Then he heard a noise.

Someone was coming his way.

Chapter Fifty-Two

GLEN PESTA KNEW WHERE HE WAS HEADED. He needed to reach the main corridor. Had to get to the maintenance room. He knew something had gone wrong during the shift change. He glanced down at his watch but couldn't read the dial in the weak red light.

He was nearing the end of the corridor when he sensed, rather than saw, somebody ahead of him. He slowed to a walk, the gun tight to his side.

"Who's there?"

As he moved closer, he could see the figure of a man. Even in the poor light, he recognized the guard's uniform. He felt the tension relax along his gun arm.

"What the hell's happening," he demanded and when the man didn't answer, didn't even turn to acknowledge him, he reached out and pushed the man roughly on the shoulder. "I'm talking to you, dammit!"

Danny Many Guns absorbed the push to his shoulder, allowing it to turn his body slightly so he stood at ninety degrees to the man with the gun.

"Mr. Pesta?" He spoke quietly.

"Yes, dammit!" Pesta snarled back.

Danny Many Guns barely moved. Just his left leg. It seemed to rise up from the floor with remarkable speed as though the hip joint was no impediment to its journey. His foot scribed a perfect arc from the floor to a point on Glen Pesta's jawline. The impact of that ascending foot smashed Pesta's jaw shut and shattered three of his back teeth. He bit through his tongue. Had there been witnesses, they would have argued about whether Pesta's feet actually left the floor. His body snapped backwards and he crashed into the opposite wall, then slid down in an awful heap to the floor.

He was out cold. Danny relieved him of his gun and his sap. For good measure, he hit him a single, fast blow to the temple.

"Glen!"

The voice came from the far end of the corridor. He moved quickly, pressed tight against the left-hand wall.

"Jesus Christ! Glen! What was that noise?"

Closer now.

Danny guessed fifty feet.

Jackson Varney peered through the narrow door opening feeling frustrated. Where the hell was that idiot son-in-law? He poured an ungrateful tirade on his son-in-law's head.

"Glen!" He was shouting now. He saw something moving down the corridor. "Glen! Is that you?"

The figure came closer. Jacko could see he was wearing prison blues.

Thank Christ for that.

"Where's Pesta?" he demanded and the guard raised his

arms by his side and dropped them.

He didn't know.

"Go find him!" Jacko snapped. "Find out what the hell's going on!"

Then the man in the corridor was right up in his face. And he could see, even in the dim red light, that something was horribly wrong.

The man's eyes didn't match. Even in the dim red light, he could see that.

"Jesus!"

Jacko tried to shut the cell door but Eddie's shoe was in the way. The man in the guard's uniform stepped inside and looked down at the cell floor. He studied the inert form of Eddie Dancer lying with his head in the paint shaker. Without looking up, he reached out. Two fingers. He touched Jacko on the neck, just above his Adam's apple. Before Jacko could snatch the man's fingers away, the man's arm seemed to twitch. Just an inch or two. It was all the power the man needed to drive his fingers in deep, shattering Jackson Varney's windpipe.

Suddenly, Jackson couldn't breath. The air in his lungs refused to leave and the air in the room refused to enter. His throat made a terrible sound, a deep animal wailing noise that seemed to go on forever. Then his brain, deprived of oxygen, began to shut down. He reached out behind him for a handhold but there was nothing to stop him as he fell backwards into darkness.

Chapter Fifty-Three

THEY TOOK ALL THREE OF US by ambulance to the Rocky-view. Me, Cindy and her daughter, Lindsay.

So they tell me.

I have little, if any, memory of the course of events. A team of experts worked on me for the next five days. And nights. I had very few visitors because of the twenty-four-hour RCMP guard on my room.

It was in that briefest of all moments, they tell me, that the paint shaker had done considerable damage. My brain was swelling. There was much discussion about brain surgery and cutting off the top of my head to give my brain an opportunity to expand, rather than crush itself to death against the inside of my skull. I believe Danny Many Guns would have removed the top of my skull with consummate skill but it was ultimately deemed unnecessary. The drugs, too many to remember, too complicated to name, had slowly worked their magic, permitting my brain to reduce back down to its normal size.

Not that I remember very much of any of it. I was so

heavily sedated, I was practically in a coma. By the fifth day, they felt confident that my still swollen brain was no longer a threat to my life. They began reducing the medication.

I came around for several hours on day six. Apparently. I still have no recollection. It was day eight before I started stringing bits and pieces together. I had a hard time remembering who was who most of the time. Some doctors were called Mister and some misters were called Doctor.

But I do remember one face.

One name that was with me throughout the entire ordeal.

Cindy Palmer.

My own Nurse Nightingale.

She was always there, swabbing what needed to be swabbed and puffing up my pillows when they needed puffing.

Danny came to see me once. We talked. He told me about the rescue. When the power went out, an automatic alarm went to the RCMP detachment. When they finally arrived, Glen Pesta's body was lying out in the main corridor, riddled with bullets. The ex-cons had extracted their own revenge before fleeing. And Jacko's body was lying in the isolation cell. He'd died from lack of oxygen. The coroner said his windpipe had collapsed, following blunt trauma.

Phillip P. Wilson had turned himself in. He had left the reservation and had done a deal with the authorities. Danny wasn't sure how the authorities wanted to handle Mr. Wilson but there seemed a good chance he might walk with time served. He wasn't sure if Wilson was getting a break for keeping quiet or if he was getting a break for telling them everything. Either way, his future looked a darn sight rosier than it had.

Danny gave me a news clipping from the *Calgary Herald*. When the RCMP finally arrived at the prison, the warden's office had been severely damaged. A huge wall safe hung open and empty.

"The ex-cons?" I asked.

"They are all farting through silk," Danny said.

I asked about Sue-Ann and Dick Wyman. Dick was driving his kids around in a brand new mini-van, so I guess everything turned out well for him too.

"How about Joe?" I asked and Danny just smiled.

"You'd think he'd won the lottery," was his only comment.

I thanked Danny Many Guns for everything he'd done for me but he merely shrugged it off.

"It's what they are for," he said.

"Who?"

"Pick-up men," he said and left as quietly as he came.

I had another visitor a few days after Danny. I was sound asleep when something wet and disgusting slobbered all over my face.

"Easy, Duke."

I opened one eye. I hardly recognized Jimmie Faddon. He was wearing thick, wrap-around dark glasses and carrying a white cane. He'd traded his Harley T-shirt and jeans for a La Costa golf shirt and chinos.

"Christ." I opened the other eye. "You found religion?"

"Fuck you." He pulled up a chair and propped his chin on his cane. "You owe me a story."

"Where're my grapes?"

"Duke ate 'em."

I ordered iced tea for two and cranked the bed up so I wasn't lying flat on my back. I recounted most of what had happened over the past couple of weeks. Jimmie was a good listener. So was Duke. He sat beside the bed resting his muzzle in my hand the whole time. I think he remembered me.

"Some story, Bro." Jimmie stood up and Duke stood beside him. "You get jammed up again, come see me."

"Did you get the bike back?"

"Len's?"

"Yeah."

He shook his head. "It's yours," he said but I couldn't take it, didn't want it. I told him where to find it.

We shook hands, palms up, interlocked thumbs, brothers-in-arms.

They left.

Duke never even looked back.

Chapter Fifty-Four

I'D BEEN TRUSSED UP in hospital for ten days. I still had two sets of IV poles, a needle in the back of each hand. The doctors told me I could expect some strange fall-out from the shaking I'd received. Headaches? Most certainly, they concluded. Probably migraines. And forgetfulness. And odd things like the hands of the clock running backwards. And body parts that might not work as well as they should.

Oh, joy.

The authorities came to see me. They grilled me night and day but I faked amnesia. Which wasn't hard. They wanted to make a federal case out of the prison break-in but couldn't find enough people on whom to hang their case. I couldn't help. I'd been out for the count when it all went down. Jacko who? Glen Pesta? Never heard of them. They questioned me about a gentleman of North American descent. They had no name to go on. I suggested Tonto but they didn't take me seriously. Finally, they threw their hands in the air and left me alone. If your memory ever comes back, they said. I assured them they'd be the first to know.

Cindy Palmer took very good care of me. I asked her how Lindsay was bearing up.

"She's tough," she said. "Like her mom."

She was spending time at her dad's house. Along with Norman, who seemed none the worse for her ordeal.

One night, after supper, I told her about Len and Doug, about how I'd smacked my shin on the paint shaker and how they'd used it on Angie. And all the other girls. I told her how Len and Doug had been beaten and had their hands chopped off.

She shivered but agreed with me that they'd gotten off lightly.

"So. What's next?" she asked when we thought I was on the mend. I told her I had an office to refurnish, a life to put back together.

But right now, I said, more than anything else, I needed a shower. "Can you stand?" she said.

I tried. But it wasn't going to happen without help.

"Hold your hands out." And she covered my hands and wrists with plastic bags, taping them to my forearms to keep the IV sites clean and dry. "Hold my arm," she said and between us, we got me to the bathroom.

I needed help lifting my legs in the tub. Then I stood up, facing her, holding onto the curtain rail, the IV poles parked close to the tub.

She was looking at me.

Then she began to giggle.

"What?"

"We forgot your gown."

I looked down. I was still wearing the pale blue hospital

gown. There was no way to take it off without removing the IVs.

"Crap. They said there'd be days like this."

She found a pair of scissors in the drawer and cut the gown off.

"You'll get in trouble," I told her.

"Phew!" She balled it up and tossed it in the wastebasket. "They'll probably promote me."

I was standing, naked, in front of her, hanging from the curtain rail. She looked me over.

"Oh dear," she said. "I'll be right back."

"Why? What do you need?"

She glanced down at me and smiled.

"More soap," she said.

And then I knew I was getting better.